JAN
HAMBRIGHT

CAMOUFLAGE
COWBOY

P7- EOS-623

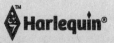

TORONTO NEW YORK LONDON
AMSTERDAM PARIS SYDNEY HAMBURG
STOCKHOLM ATHENS TOKYO MILAN MADRID
PRAGUE WARSAW BUDAPEST AUCKLAND

Special thanks and acknowledgment to Jan Hambright for her contribution to the Daddy Corps series.

Recycling programs
for this product may
not exist in your area.

ISBN-13: 978-0-373-69578-2

CAMOUFLAGE COWBOY

www.Harlequin.com

Printed in U.S.A.

"I want you and Caleb to stay for as long as it takes."

Grace stared at him, feeling the heat in his touch as it pulsed along her arm in an intimate connection she could feel growing between them.

"I'll find a way to neutralize the creep stalking you." There was absolute seriousness in the set of Nick's mouth and the slight narrowing of his intense blue eyes.

A blade of fear knifed through her. "Be careful, Nick. He's got friends with badges who don't seem to mind helping him. He's been able to trace me everywhere I've been for the past three years."

"That's when you ran?"

"Yes."

"Who is he, Grace?"

Her emotions locked up, strangled with tension that wound tight like a cord inside of her. The whole truth could drive Nick away when she needed his help the most, but she couldn't live with herself if she let him walk into a trap because he hadn't been forewarned.

"He's my ex-brother-in-law."

"Your ex-husband's brother?"

"My dead husband's brother."

ABOUT THE AUTHOR

Jan Hambright penned her first novel at seventeen, but claims it was pure rubbish. However, it did open the door on her love for storytelling. Born in Idaho, she resides there with her husband, three of their five children, a three-legged watchdog and a spoiled horse named Texas, who always has time to listen to her next story idea while they gallop along.

A self-described adrenaline junkie, Jan spent ten years as a volunteer EMT in rural Idaho, and jumped out of an airplane at ten thousand feet attached to a man with a parachute, just to celebrate turning forty. Now she hopes to make your adrenaline level rise along with that of her danger-seeking characters. She would like to hear from her readers and hopes you enjoy the story world she has created for you. Jan can be reached at P.O. Box 2537, McCall, Idaho 83638.

Books by Jan Hambright

HARLEQUIN INTRIGUE
865—RELENTLESS
943—ON FIRE
997—SHOWDOWN WITH THE SHERIFF
1040—AROUND-THE-CLOCK PROTECTOR
1118—THE HIGH COUNTRY RANCHER
1141—THE PHANTOM OF BLACK'S COVE
1219—KEEPING WATCH
1233—CHRISTMAS COUNTDOWN
1311—CAMOUFLAGE COWBOY

CAST OF CHARACTERS

Nick Cavanaugh—A former army ranger and member of Corps Security and Investigations, Nick is grateful for the second chance he has been given by CSaI founder Bart Bellows. But the object of his special assignment, Grace Marshall, could prove to be his toughest mission yet.

Grace Marshall—Given up for adoption as an infant, Grace is now desperate to find her birth mother in order to save her ill son's life via a bone marrow transplant. Can she locate the woman before time runs out for her little boy, Caleb, and before a maniac from her past threatens both of their lives?

Caleb Marshall—Four-year-old Caleb was born with aplastic anemia. He needs a donor, but his rare blood type has narrowed his chances of finding a suitable match. Can one be found in time?

Wes Bradley—The soldier was reported killed in Iraq by an IED, but his name has surfaced in connection with some of the attacks against Governor Lila Lockhart. Could he still be alive?

Rodney Marshall—Bent on vengeance, he's determined to make Grace Marshall pay for what she did.

Governor Lila Lockhart—Texas loves her, but a scandal from her past could destroy her chance of ever becoming the president of the United States. Only Nick Cavanaugh, her hand-picked CSaI agent, stands between the discovery of that truth and the highest office in the land.

Chapter One

Nick Cavanaugh rose from one of the park benches perched on the perimeter of Freedom's town square, checked the traffic in both directions and jaywalked across Main Street, careful to keep his pace nonchalant.

Anticipation skated over his nerves, etching certainty into his brain. He'd learned it hard and solid on the battlefields of Iraq: stay one step ahead of your enemies, or two steps back for a clear shot.

His heart rate notched up.

The door of Potter's Drugstore swept open just as Nick made the curb half a block to the east.

Funny. His target didn't look like much of a threat. The observation gelled in his brain as he watched her step out into the early afternoon sunlight. She casually looped her arm in her purse strap and deposited it on her shoulder. She turned to her right and moved along the sidewalk, her blond ponytail swaying back and forth between her shoulder blades as she moved away from him.

Nick increased his rate of follow, backing off only when she paused in front of the Talk of the Town Café to study something in the window before proceeding due north again.

He knew her beat-up silver Toyota Camry was sucked up next to the curb half a block away.

Tension braided his muscles into a knot. Had he pegged her correctly? Or was he headed for an ambush? He wrestled the questions to the back of his mind and looked at his watch. *C'mon, c'mon,* he thought. He had to get to Grace Marshall now. Another minute and she'd make it to her car and escape.

Focused on her alone, he narrowed the distance.

On his left, a man wearing a black hoodie, black sweatpants and running shoes brushed past him and broke into a sprint.

Time slowed as Nick listened to the jogger's pounding footsteps echo off the sidewalk and ping against the brick-and-mortar storefronts that lined the quaint main street of Freedom, Texas.

Grace Marshall's high-pitched shriek slammed against his eardrums. The man in the black hoodie and Grace were engaged in a tug of war over the purse.

"Hey! Leave her alone!" Nick took aim at the would-be purse-snatcher and charged.

Stressed, the metal ring anchoring the strap to the purse broke.

Grace still clutched the handbag, but the force of the sudden release sent the bag flopping across the sidewalk as the strap slipped through the purse-snatcher's fingers.

He took off down the street at a dead run and vanished around the corner at 4th and Main.

Car keys, pill bottles, a hairbrush and a wallet were scattered across the sidewalk next to her. She went to her knees on the concrete.

Nick shuffled to a stop and knelt beside her.

"I saw what happened. Are you okay?"

She turned wide blue eyes on him for a second before reaching for the contents of her purse. "Yeah."

He reached out and picked up one of the prescription pill bottles, glanced at the name on it, then handed it to her. "I'll call the police. I got a good look at him. I think I can give them a description—"

"No! I mean…" Grace tried to force the lump in her throat to go down, but it wouldn't budge. The last thing she needed was local law enforcement poking around in her business. "I still have my purse and its contents. There's no reason to involve the police. He's probably halfway to the next county by now." She shoved the last item into her handbag and pulled the zipper closed before staring eye to eye with the handsome stranger who'd come to her rescue.

His irises were electric blue, his stare leveled on her with pulse-zapping heat that made her cheeks light up. "But thank you for offering. I'm not sure I could have held on much longer. If you hadn't spooked him, he might have gotten away with this." She squeezed the brown leather bag she gripped like a lifeline and realized her hands were shaking uncontrollably. "Oh. I don't feel so good."

Concern crossed his features and settled around his mouth in the granite-hard line of his lips. She was suddenly sure this man, if asked, could and would trail the thug to hell and back.

"Come on. Let's get you inside somewhere." He stood up and helped her stand by putting his arm around her waist. Pulling free from him wasn't as option, she realized as her stomach roiled, roiled again and settled down with several deep gulps of air.

Perhaps she should have eaten breakfast…or lunch

for that matter, but her son Caleb's treatment days were always like this. Next time she'd be sure to put a banana or something in her purse.

"I've got somewhere I need to be." Her declaration seemed to fall on deaf ears as he steered her toward the door of the café.

"You're suffering from mild shock. It'll pass in the time it takes you to let me buy you a cup of coffee."

She couldn't argue with his assessment. Her knees trembled, her feet tingled, and if his strong arm weren't wrapped tightly around her waist, she wasn't sure she'd be standing right now. She had half an hour before she had to pick Caleb up, and Holy Cross Hospital was only ten minutes away. She could make it in plenty of time.

"You're right. I suppose the surprise of almost having my arm jerked off by a stranger is a good reason to sit down for a minute."

"I knew you'd see it my way." He chuckled deep in his throat, a soothing male sound that made her smile as he reached out with his free hand and pulled open the door to Talk of the Town Café.

She stepped inside, absorbing its cool retro 1950s interior, complete with red-and-white upholstered booth seats, and a black-and-white checkerboard tile floor. It was a novelty she could get used to—if the Help Wanted sign in the window managed to come down after she applied for the job. And maybe, if she were lucky, the man with his arm around her would come in every once in a while so she could buy him a cup of coffee as thanks.

Nick zeroed in on a booth in the rear of the establishment, away from the noise of the regular afternoon crowd.

This was his orchestrated break in his assignment,

and he didn't plan to waste an iota of it. He might not get another chance at a one-on-one conversation with the target of his investigation.

The café's owner, Faith Scott, waved to him from behind the counter and raised the steaming coffeepot in her hand.

He nodded and grudgingly let go of Grace to help her into the booth's seat before taking a spot across from her with his back to the room.

"Coffee?" Faith had already turned their cups upright in their saucers before Nick realized he was staring at the woman sitting across from him.

"Yes. Please. And for you?"

"Just water, no ice," Grace said. "I'm not sure my nerves could handle a shot of caffeine right now."

He watched a tentative smile curve her full lips as she considered him through eyes tinted a shade-of-heaven blue. This wasn't the army way of conducting an interrogation, but he couldn't help enjoying the view.

"Would you like a piece of pie? I just took a cinnamon-apple-crumb out of the oven ten minutes ago," Faith said from next to their table.

Nick broke eye contact with Grace Marshall and immediately felt his blood pressure drop a fraction. "Not for me, but maybe…" He glanced back at Grace, anxious to prompt her response. "I'm sorry, I don't know your name."

"Grace."

"Maybe Grace would like a piece."

She shook her head. "No, thank you. I've got to run in a few minutes."

"I'll get your water." Faith turned and headed for the counter, leaving them alone in silence.

Reaching across the table, he extended his hand to her. "I'm Nick Cavanaugh." The moment she put her delicate palm into his, a jolt radiated through him. "I don't believe I've seen you around Freedom before."

Her gaze dropped for an instant. "I spend most of my time at home, or at work."

He released his grasp and leaned back into the booth seat just as Faith put a glass of water in front of Grace.

"Thanks," she whispered, locking her fingers around it for an instant before raising it to her mouth and taking several deep swallows.

Nick sensed her caution, saw it in the way her nails blanched against the glass in her hand as she lowered it to the table.

Trust. He needed to establish a level of trust between them, and fast. He was losing her with every tick of the second hand on his watch, and for some reason, that mattered to him.

Rocking slightly to the left, he dug into his pants pocket and pulled out his wallet. "I know you've got to leave soon, but I want you to have this just in case you need to contact me." He opened his billfold and pulled out a Corps Security and Investigations card with his name and cell number on it.

"If you change your mind and want me to describe the purse-snatcher to the police, just give me a call at this number." He slid the card across the table to her.

She picked it up and stared at it for a moment before nonchalantly putting it in her sweater pocket. "Thank you, but that won't be necessary. I'm fine. I have my purse, and its contents. It might be better if we drop the matter entirely."

Curiosity jetted across Nick's mind and he focused

his gaze on Grace's beautiful face. How was it she'd managed to avoid giving him anything more than her first name? Sure, he had an entire paper file amassed on her: he knew where she worked, where she lived, what she drove and damn near what she'd had for dinner last night, but his desire to glean it from her own lips was falling flat. The woman was playing it safe, a fact that intrigued him and bothered him at the same time. What was she hiding?

"I really need to get going." She took another quick swallow from her glass, put it down, snagged her purse and slid out of the booth.

"Thanks again for your help, Nick." She gave him a sweet smile, turned and walked to the café counter, where she spoke to Faith Scott for a moment.

Nick turned slightly, watching Faith reach under the counter and pull out a sheet of paper, hand it to Grace, then return to her customers.

He turned back around and waited for the jingle of the bell on the café door to signal Grace's departure from the establishment.

Reaching into his jean jacket, he pulled an evidence bag out of the inside pocket. Grace may be tight-lipped with personal information, but DNA held no such pretenses, and he planned to make a mitochondrial comparison with the sample the governor had already given him. He grasped the glass at the bottom where she hadn't touched it, dumped the remainder of the water into her unused coffee cup and eased the glass into the bag.

"Uh-huh."

The sound of a throat being cleared raked over Nick's nerves. He stared up at Faith and the coffeepot in her hand.

"What are you up to, Nick?" she asked as she topped off his java.

"I could tell you, but then I'd have to kill you."

She grinned. "Does this have anything to do with your secret assignment for Governor Lockhart?"

Nick shook his head and slipped out of the booth. "You know the things we do at CSaI are hush-hush." He winked at her as he tucked the evidence bag inside his jacket. As long as no one knew what that assignment was, the secret was safe.

"That's stealing, Cavanaugh."

"Not if I bring it back. Washed."

Faith shook her head and grinned. "I'll believe it when I see it."

"While we're telling secrets—" Nick pulled out his wallet and put a five on the table "—mind if I ask what you gave Grace at the counter a moment ago?"

"That's no secret. Molly Alden left for college months ago. Gloria and I have been taking up the slack, but between taking care of Kaleigh and adjusting to having a man around again, I'm pooped. I need someone to fill in a couple nights a week. I gave Grace an application. I just hope she fills it out and gets it back to me. I like her."

Nick grinned. Faith had recently won the heart of fellow CSaI agent and friend Matt Soarez. "I'd offer to help around here, but I'm not sure some of your regulars wouldn't break me and cause me to spill the state secrets I have along with their coffee."

"Stan Lorry and Fred March could probably pull it off," Faith said with a chuckle, referring to her cranky elderly regulars. "The trouble would come when they told Allen Davidson and he aired it on his radio show."

Nick did a fake shudder. "Spooky. I'll see you later." He headed for the door and stepped outside, where he immediately spotted the top of Grace's head as she ducked into her car half a block up the street.

He fell into an easy stroll as she pulled away from the curb, headed due north. Probably to the hospital was his guess. He'd learned that she had a four-year-old son named Caleb who received some sort of treatments at Holy Cross every couple of weeks. The prescription drug bottle had confirmed it, but there were holes in Grace's background history. Holes he'd yet to plug.

The sound of a revved engine caught his attention as he spotted a late-model black sedan with Montana license plates pull away from the curb and roll in a car's length behind Grace.

Caution raked over his nerves. From his observation point on the park bench earlier, he'd seen the same car just after she'd arrived. Come to think of it, he hadn't seen the driver exit the vehicle.

He took a right onto 4th Street and dug the keys to his pickup out of his pocket. Was it possible the beautiful and cautious Grace Marshall was being followed by someone other than him? He decided to keep an eye out in order to confirm his suspicion.

NICK WALKED INTO Corps Security and Investigations headquarters still mulling over his and Grace Marshall's brief encounter.

Harlan McClain sat behind his desk minus the black hoodie and sweatpants he'd used to disguise himself for the purse-snatching ruse.

"Thanks, buddy," Nick said as he tossed his keys onto

his desk and leaned against the edge. "Your timing was spot-on."

Harlan swiveled his desk chair. "Did you get what you needed from her?"

"Yeah." He reached inside his jacket and pulled out the evidence bag. Holding it up to the light streaming in through one of the loft windows, he could see the clear imprint of Grace Marshall's lips on the rim of the glass. Grace's lips. Her perfect, kissable lips.

"You're not going to tell me what the hell is going on, are you?" Harlan rocked forward to rest his elbows on his knees.

"Can't, but suffice to say it's an assignment that came down personally from Governor Lockhart." Nick put the bag down on his desk and went around to the other side. He pulled open the file drawer, took out a lab form and sat down in his chair. The results of the DNA test on the lip impression would come in from their private lab in a week. It was the definitive piece of evidence he needed. He didn't particularly like the method he'd been forced to use to obtain it, but in this case, the end did justify the means, and he'd be able to tell the governor conclusively whether or not Grace Marshall was her illegitimate daughter.

Nick filled out the paperwork, aware of the modulation of Nolan Law's voice as he stepped out of his office, still talking on his cell phone.

"Is he awake yet?" A measure of excitement materialized in Nolan's tone. They'd yet to catch a break in the case of a shooting at Governor Lockhart's ranch, and their only link was Trevor Lewis, a man lying in the ICU, breathing with the help of a ventilator. The man

Harlan McClain had so expertly perforated before he'd been able to hurt Stacy Giordano.

Nick looked up, watching Nolan pace back and forth as he talked to the team member assigned to guard Trevor Lewis, their only suspect in the war someone had instituted against Governor Lila Lockhart and her bid for the U.S. presidency.

"Who's watching Lewis today?" Nick asked Harlan.

"Matteo. I take over at five."

"Is Lewis still on a ventilator?" Nick turned in his chair to face his fellow team member.

"Yeah, but the doc is going to wake him up around four this afternoon. Nolan wants us there so we can persuade him to give up the name of the shooter who infiltrated the party at Twin Harts Ranch wearing a stolen deputy's uniform. We need to nab the guy before he tries again."

Nick couldn't agree more, but he'd been an outsider on the case from the start. Forced instead to focus on his special assignment for the governor.

Nolan closed his phone and headed toward them. "Let's go. The doctor told Matteo that Lewis is stable enough to breathe on his own. He's going to remove the tube. He'll give us five minutes to get some answers before they prep him for medical transport to the hospital in Amarillo."

Anticipation clung to Nick's nerves as he taped the lab request to the evidence bag and stood up, then on a whim, he picked up his pen and put an X next to the fingerprint-lift request, as well. Maybe Grace's prints on the water glass could lead him to the holes in her life story if he decided to run them.

CSaI receptionist Amelia Bond glanced up from

behind her desk near the front entrance, catching wind of the hustle being stirred up as Nolan hurried for the door.

On the way out, Nick put the evidence bag on Amelia's desk for processing. He knew her efficiency would have the sample out today and the results back to him before he could stop thinking about Grace Marshall's perfect lip impression on the edge of the glass.

Chapter Two

Nick pulled his vehicle in next to Nolan Law's sleek black Mercedes. He'd never cared much for hospitals, cared even less for them now. He'd seen too many men perish in them and had come close to being a casualty himself not too long ago—before CSaI founder Bart Bellows gave him a reason to breathe again.

The hair on the back of his neck bristled as he climbed out and locked his pickup. He took a quick scan of the parking lot, searching for the source of the hinky feeling climbing all over his nerves. They were being watched. He'd bet his best horse on it.

A pair of nurses chatted as they walked toward the main entrance to Holy Cross Hospital. A single male dressed in green scrubs was in the process of getting into his car while he held a cell phone plastered to his ear and spoke into it at just below a yell.

Nick's stare locked on Grace Marshall's beat-up silver Camry parked in a slot near the front doors. He hadn't anticipated coming in contact with her here. Still, he wasn't sure he could attribute her presence as the source of his agitation.

He fell in behind Nolan and Harlan, keeping his senses on high alert as they headed for the main entrance. Trevor Lewis hadn't acted alone, and Nick couldn't help but feel no one was safe in Freedom until his accomplice was identified and captured. He wouldn't relax until they were inside the hospital and out of the open.

The double set of extra-wide automatic doors ground open and Nick's gaze connected with Grace Marshall's on the other side of the gap. A moment of recognition passed between them and she smiled.

Nolan and Harlan walked past her, headed for the elevator bank on the opposite side of the hospital's lobby. A wave of attraction swelled inside of Nick as he approached Grace and stopped.

"Grace." He focused a degree of surprise in his voice. He was glad that Harlan had ditched the black hoodie and sweats. He was convinced that along with her level of caution there was no doubt a level of observation she practiced on a regular basis.

"Nick Cavanaugh. I had no idea you were following me."

A stream of guilt flooded his insides, but he forded it with a grin. The elevator bell chimed in the background and he glanced up to where Nolan and Harlan waited for him. Making eye contact with Harlan, he nodded slightly, certain that Harlan had recognized his purse-snatching target from earlier in the afternoon and was more than happy to duck for cover inside the elevator.

"I'm checking in on someone. Visiting hours and all." He took the opportunity to look down at the little boy sitting in the wheelchair that Grace had been pushing to the exit, and now clung to.

Her sweet smile faded as she reached down to brush

her hand across the top of the little boy's head. "Caleb, this is Mr. Nick Cavanaugh. Nick, this is my son, Caleb."

"Hey, buddy." He bent over, reached out and grasped the little boy's hand, giving it a gentle shake. The child's line of sight started at his boot-clad feet, went up his jean-encased legs and eventually ended with Caleb staring up at him with eyes the same heavenly blue as his mother's.

"Are you a cowboy, Mister Nick?"

Nick straightened, amused by the little boy's power of observation. "Hmm. Yeah. You could say I'm a cowboy."

"Gotta horse?"

"A few."

"Can I ride one? My friend Zachary-G says it's fun. He rides horses all the time."

Caution raked over Nick's nerves. He hadn't considered the connection that might exist between Zachary Giordano and Caleb Marshall. They did both attend Cradles to Crayons, and Grace did work there part-time as a preschool teacher. Maybe he should have enlisted another team member besides Harlan McClain to pull off the ruse, but hindsight was always twenty-twenty.

"Maybe sometime your mom will bring you out to the ranch and I'll saddle one up for you."

"Really?" Caleb's eyes widened to the size of silver dollars. "Wait till I tell Zachary-G!"

The air was suddenly charged with vibes Nick could almost feel. He straightened, dialing in on Grace's face, on the way she pressed her lips together as if she were about to cry. His heart twisted in his chest. Instinctively he reached out and brushed his hand against her upper arm—a mistake, he realized, when a jolt of heat passed between them. She pulled away.

"Let me." He was glad when she stepped aside and allowed him to take the handles of the wheelchair. "Where's your car?"

She pointed to the Camry and fell in next to him as they pushed through the sliding doors, across the breezeway and out into the parking lot.

Caleb began to hum, his tiny voice picking up the vibrations from the asphalt as the wheelchair wheels bumped over the uneven surface.

Nick swallowed hard, sucked into the emotion coming from the woman next to him. Caleb Marshall was a very sick little boy. How sick? He didn't know. But he intended to find out.

"Here we are, tiger."

Grace moved past them to unlock the car, then pulled the right rear passenger-side door open.

Nick eased the chair to a stop, stepped around to the front, squatted down and flipped up the footrest pads. "Need some help?" he asked, studying Caleb's handsome little-boy face.

"Nope." Determination gripped Caleb's features as he put his tennis-shoe-encased feet firmly on the ground, grasped the armrests and pushed up from the seat, where he promptly wobbled and fell forward into Nick's arms.

Grace let out an audible gasp and was next to them in a heartbeat. "Caleb, you know you need to take it easy after your treatment."

"I want to do it myself."

"Come on, buddy, I'll help you." As if he were holding a fragile sheet of glass, Nick guided Caleb into the backseat of his mother's car and supervised him as he buckled himself in his car seat.

"What color is your horse, Mister Nick?" he asked,

staring with a huge grin on his face. "I wanna tell Zachary-G."

"He's a bay."

"Bay?"

"It's a reddish-brown color, with a black mane and tail. Beautiful."

Caleb nodded and laid his head back against the seat. "A bay," he said again as he closed his eyes. "Red-brown."

Nick stepped back and closed the car door before turning to face Grace.

"Thank you," she whispered, some of the tension visibly leaving her body in a shoulder shrug. "He always overestimates his strength after every transfusion. It takes a day or so for him to bounce back."

"You can't fault him for trying."

She swallowed and shook her head. "Sometimes I marvel at his will to survive, to go until he can't go anymore."

"What's wrong with him, Grace?" Caution brought her chin up as she studied him and he witnessed the battle between suspicion and trust as it warred across her delicate features and settled in her blue eyes.

"He needs a bone-marrow transplant. He has aplastic anemia and has to have a blood transfusion every two weeks, but his doctor informed me this afternoon that his condition is worsening. We need to find a bone-marrow donor as soon as possible or he's going to..." Her voice faltered.

Die? Nick mentally finished the horrific statement and reached out for her, folding his arms around her slender shoulders. Sympathy leeched from his insides, but he felt her stiffen and pull away.

"I'm sorry," she whispered. "This isn't any of your concern." She went around to the driver-side door. "But thank you for your help." She climbed into the car and fired the engine.

Nick stepped back as she maneuvered out of the parking space and drove away. He stared after her for a moment, snagged the empty wheelchair and turned for the hospital entrance.

Grace Marshall was clearly desperate. Hell, he'd be desperate, too, if he had a dying child, but desperate people did desperate things. Was it possible the donor she was seeking for Caleb was the governor? He didn't know much about donor matches, but Lila Lockhart stood a good chance of being a blood relative to Caleb Marshall.

Worry needled him all the way back into the hospital and followed him into the elevator. Was it possible Grace knew the governor could be her birth mother? Was she willing to blackmail Lila into donating bone marrow to her dying grandson, or she'd…she'd what? Sabotage Lila's shot at a presidential bid?

Nick's sense of right had gone into battle with his sense of duty by the time he stepped off the elevator on the third-floor ICU unit and into the jaws of chaos.

"Code blue…code blue. Paging Dr. Karnahan, Dr. Mark Karnahan to ICU, stat." The request rang out over the unit's PA system.

Nick sidestepped a nurse as she rushed a lifesaving crash cart down the corridor to where Nolan and Harlan stood in the hallway. She spoke with them for an instant before wheeling it past them and into the room. Trevor Lewis's room.

Nick hurried toward them. "Nolan! What's going on?"

Nolan Law shook his head, his gaze going to the floor for an instant before he made eye contact again. "Lewis coded. One minute he'd agreed to tell us who the shooter was at the governor's ranch, and the next I was performing CPR."

"I'm sorry, sir." Nick's blood churned in apprehension. Trevor Lewis had been stable up until this point. Stable enough to talk. Was it possible someone had a hand in changing his condition so he'd never say another word? What if that someone had been the source of the hinky feeling Nick had had in the parking lot when they'd first arrived?

Nick got his bearings in the east-west hallway and bolted for the window at the end of the corridor overlooking the parking lot below. Nolan and Harlan followed close behind.

"What's going on?" Nolan asked from next to him as he stared out of the window three floors above the myriad of cars.

"I should have said something, but when we arrived, I had the feeling we were being watched." Nick put his focus on a man jogging through the lot wearing blue scrubs and a tan jacket with the hood pulled up. "There."

"I'll be damned," Harlan said. "We passed him getting into the elevator when we got off." Harlan banged his fist against the ledge in frustration. "I barely got a look at him with his head down."

They watched the man disappear into a bank of trees and shrubs on the outer perimeter of the parking lot. There wasn't a chance they could catch him at this point.

"We better hope Trevor Lewis survives, because he's our only link right now." Nolan pushed away from the window, but Nick and Harlan remained, picking out each car that moved from its space on the tree-lined street beyond the hospital entrance.

"Red compact...Ford Focus. Dark-gray SUV...Tahoe. Black pickup...Dodge." Nick called out the vehicles. "White...pickup...Dodge." Anyone in a hurry to clear the area would be long gone by now, but odds were if he'd driven away from the scene in the past ten minutes they'd have a make on what he drove.

Harlan wrote the last vehicle description down on the small notepad he held in his hand. "It's a long shot, but I'll see if Sheriff Hale will plug the makes and models into the system. Maybe we'll get lucky."

"We don't even know if the guy drove a car. He could have been on foot the entire time, could have been standing in this very window when we arrived and timed his escape accordingly. I'm going to check and see if the hospital security cameras caught a visual of his face at some point."

Harlan nodded. "I can tell you he was tall...six foot, give or take an inch. Powerful build. I'll see if any hits on the autos produce an owner who matches his physical description."

"Let's hope we catch a break." Nick glanced down the corridor at the empty chair next to the entrance of Trevor Lewis's room and realized he hadn't seen Matteo. "Where's Matt?"

"He wasn't here when Nolan and I arrived. The charge nurse said she saw him head for the vending room to grab a soda."

"That takes what, three minutes? He should be back by now. Let's have a look."

Together, he and Harlan hustled along the hallway, focused on the vending-machine cubical on the right at the end of the corridor, marked by an information sign hanging above the entrance.

He had a bad feeling about this. First Trevor Lewis; now Matteo? What the hell was going on?

Nick slowed his pace, raised his right hand and motioned Harlan to the other side of the entrance before he sucked up next to the door frame and glanced inside.

The small room was empty except for a row of soda and snack machines ablaze in fluorescent light.

"Nothing," Harlan said, shrugging his shoulders. "I don't know how, but he must have gotten past us."

Relaxing his stance, Nick stepped through the entrance and surveyed the room for hidden nooks and crannies, still unable to shake the worry surging in his veins. Where was Matteo Soarez? He'd never leave his post.

Frustrated, Nick pulled out his cell phone and dialed Matt's number.

Over the drone of the machines, he swore he heard a muffled ringtone. "Do you hear that, Harlan?"

Harlan stopped in his tracks. "Yeah."

"Where's it coming from?" A wave of desperation floated Nick along the bank of vending machines as he listened to the familiar ringtone grow louder. At the end of the processional, a cooler filled with premade sandwiches stood silent and dark. Unplugged?

In an instant, reality jolted through Nick on the heels of one last ringtone before a beep signaled one missed call.

"Damn," he whispered as he stared into the corner between the cooler and the wall. Into the narrow gap where Matteo Soarez was crushed against the wall with a black hood over his head.

"It's Matt! Help me move this!" Nick and Harlan worked in unison, holding on to the cumbersome machine, pulling and rocking it until the space opened several inches.

Nick reached in and snagged Matt's limp arm where it hung at his side.

"Matt, buddy. Can you hear me?"

Matteo groaned.

A good sign in Nick's mind. "We're going to get you out of there. Hold on."

Harlan jockeyed the cooler case, opening the crack another inch, just enough that Nick felt Matt's body give in the tight space.

"That's it! A little more." Inch by inch, he dragged Matteo out of the crevice and lowered him to the floor.

Fingering the knot of cord that held the bag in place over Matt's head, Nick prayed that it hadn't also strangled his buddy in the process. How long had he been pinned? How long had he been deprived of oxygen?

The knot came free and together he and Harlan pulled the bag off Matteo's head. He blinked against the overhead lights and mumbled underneath the strip of duct tape over his mouth.

Peeling up an edge, Nick stripped the tape off. Matteo let out a stream of profanity that echoed against the walls of the cubical. "Are you okay?" Nick asked, staring at the blazing red mark around Matt's mouth and the taser burn on his neck.

"I'll live."

"What happened?" Harlan rocked back onto the floor.

"Somebody jumped me from behind." Matt sucked in three gulps of air in a row and sat up. "Got me with a Taser, shoved me into the corner and proceeded to squash me like a grape."

"Did you get a look at him?" Nick rose to his feet; Harlan followed. Bending down, they each put an arm around Matteo and helped him stand.

"No. It happened too damn fast. One minute my soda was dropping, the next it was me. I did get one punch in, but it felt like I'd slugged an oak."

"Big guy, huh?" Speculation laced through Nick's mind. The description of a powerful perpetrator coincided with Harlan's description of the man he'd seen getting into the elevator. "Could be the guy we saw running across the parking lot."

Together they helped Matteo out into the corridor.

"I've got this," Matt said as he got his legs working and shrugged off their help. "What's up with Lewis?" He nodded toward the commotion down the hall.

"Coded half an hour ago. They're working to save his life right now." Nick spotted Nolan gesturing in their direction. "Come on. Maybe they've revived him."

They walked back down the corridor and stopped next to Nolan in the doorway of Trevor Lewis's room. He looked up and shook his head, his mouth set in a grim line.

From inside, behind a privacy curtain, Nick clearly heard a male voice above the hum of a heart monitor and the whoosh of air being forced into Trevor Lewis's lungs through a bag valve mask.

"Stop CPR. Check the monitor."

"Still a flat line, Dr. Karnahan."

"I'm going to call it. Time of death, 5:41 p.m."

Chapter Three

Nick fidgeted in his chair as he glanced around the conference table at the CSaI team members: Nolan Law, Parker McKenna, Matteo Soarez, Wade Coltrane and Harlan McClain. They were all officially in battle mode after the events at Holy Cross Hospital, and their motto—For Country; For Brotherhood; For Love— never rang more true. Too bad their boss and mentor, Bart Bellows, was out sick, battling a persistent case of bronchitis.

He swallowed, trying to alleviate the knot of gratitude that squeezed in his chest. He had Bart to thank, along with every man sitting at the table right now. Because of them, he was almost whole again. He reined in his emotions and tried to focus on the case at hand. Trevor Lewis's autopsy report was decisive. He'd been injected with a large dose of potassium chloride, enough to stop an elephant's heart, and the hospital's surveillance footage had confirmed the man they'd seen running across the parking lot had been in Lewis's room moments before Nolan and Harlan arrived. He'd also been the one who followed Matt into the vending-machine room and tried to make him a human pancake with a sandwich cooler.

"None of the vehicles Nick and I spotted came back with an owner who matched the perpetrator's height and build. We've got nothing." Harlan leaned back in his chair.

"So what do we know about Trevor Lewis, other than someone wanted him dead before he could talk to us?" Nolan Law questioned from his seat at the head of the table where Bart usually sat.

"From a simple background check we know he spent a couple of years in Iraq," team member Wade Coltrane said. "Other than that, he's flown under the radar. Sheriff Hale has agreed to release Lewis's personal effects to us tomorrow morning since no one has come forward to claim them. It includes his cell phone. We should be able to find out who he's been communicating with. If we get lucky, a name will pop."

Nolan nodded. "Good work. Parker, I want you, Matteo and Harlan to double your protection and surveillance efforts on Governor Lockhart. She's planning to spend a considerable amount of time this month out at Twin Harts Ranch rather than in Austin. She'll be here right up until Thanksgiving. Bart has given us carte blanche to do whatever it takes to keep her and those around her safe." Nolan shoved his paperwork into a folder and stood up.

"Nick's working on a special assignment for the governor, but he'll fill in where needed on this case. Everyone, stay on your toes. We're dealing with a determined individual here, and I don't have to tell you how unpredictable someone like that can be."

A mutual round of agreement prevailed in the room as each team member gathered their paperwork and their thoughts.

"I want you all back here at 0600 hours on Monday morning to cover discovery and a plan of action." Everyone filed out of the conference room.

Nick took up the rear and flipped the lights off on his way out. He needed to grab a bite to eat before he headed out to his special reconnaissance assignment. He'd been monitoring Grace Marshall's movements for the past week since seeing her and Caleb at Holy Cross. She was predictable, but she'd yet to make any attempt to contact Governor Lila Lockhart with a blackmail demand, and considering Caleb's health situation was growing more desperate with each passing day, he expected her to make a move soon. That was, if she knew the governor's identity....

GRACE GLANCED IN HER REARVIEW mirror, her stare focused on the headlights of the black sedan following her an eighth of a mile back. A knot cinched in her stomach. She'd seen the vehicle several times this week, but had never gotten a look at the driver inside. Now she was sure the same car had pulled in behind her as she left the parking lot behind the Talk of the Town Café after turning in her employment application to Faith Scott.

There was really only one way to find out.

She stepped down on the gas pedal. The car picked up speed. Hesitation tempered the caution ricocheting around inside of her, but she had to be sure. She couldn't risk having her and Caleb's trail picked up again. Not when she was sure she was close to finding the only woman in Freedom who might be able to save Caleb's life.

Glancing at the gas gauge, she watched the needle bobbing near a quarter of a tank. How far could she go? How fast could she run before her past caught up with her?

Caleb's voice reached her ears from where he played with his toy truck in the backseat. He sputtered and rumbled, imitating the noise of the motor as the truck made a fictitious trail across his knees and up his leg. The screech of a sudden stop, before the rumbling resumed.

She couldn't let her son down. Not when she was so close.

If she could lose the car and driver in the confusing confines of the Chisholm Trail subdivision, she could backtrack and make it home undetected. She couldn't risk ever letting Rodney Marshall get as close to them as he had in Amarillo.

The speedometer climbed as she floored the Camry and raced out of town, past the turn that would have taken her to her condo complex.

Gearing down into Third without touching her brake pedal just like she'd practiced, Grace made the sweeping corner into the subdivision without slowing. Ahead of her on the road she could see a set of taillights similar to her Camry's.

The squeal of brakes behind her made her heartbeat kick up a notch and the car's taillights screamed red in her left peripheral. He'd failed to anticipate her quick move. It would take him thirty seconds to turn around.

Buoyed by her success, she took a hard right and killed the car's lights as she aimed for the eastern side of the subdivision with its rows upon rows of unfinished homes and dark streetlamps.

She'd taken the route a hundred times during the day.

Memorized every turn, so she could use it to evade him if the day ever came. That day was here.

In her rearview mirror she saw the black sedan zip past as she made the corner and drove parallel with him, but she didn't let up. She would only have a few minutes before he discovered she'd given him the slip.

Gearing down into Second, Grace turned at the fifth house on the right and shot past the unfinished garage and onto the worn path that led across a field and onto her street.

Hope stirred inside of her, but it was quickly dashed when she spotted a set of car lights coming around the corner on the north end of the street.

Silently she prayed the dust rolling out behind her would settle before he could pick up her trail.

Focused on the last hundred feet, she nosed the car in between the first couple of condo units and drove out onto the paved street. Turning sharply to the right she reached up and hit her garage-door opener before gearing down to a crawl and slipping inside. Only then did she apply the brakes and hit the close button. She didn't take a deep breath until she heard the overhead door lock in place behind her.

"Where's the light, Mommy?" Caleb's tiny voice sliced through the fear holding her in place. She released her seat belt and turned toward him.

"In a minute, I'll turn it on. Can you hold on?" She reached out and touched her son's leg to reassure him. She wasn't sure how determined the maniac following her was, but even a hint of light could alert him to their location inside of the garage.

"Yeah."

"Good boy." She patted his leg and listened to him start up his toy-truck sounds again.

Above the rumbling, she listened, but it was the brief flash of light outside in the street that made every muscle in her body tense.

Had he discovered where they lived? Fear slid down her spine and spilled into her body. Rodney Marshall had vowed to kill her for what she'd done. She didn't doubt that he would, if he got the chance.

Chilled to the bone, Grace shuddered and shoved her hands into the pockets of her sweater, where she came in contact with the business card Nick Cavanaugh had given her at the café a week ago. She closed her fingers around it and slowly pulled it out of its hiding place.

Maybe there was hope after all.

WHAT THE…? NICK HELD his position, curiosity welding him to the spot. He'd parked his pickup on Grace's street of identical condo units, one after another, until they all looked the same. He'd seen her car roll past him without the headlights on, then slow and disappear into the open garage compartment of her condo unit.

The door had instantly come down, moments before he spotted lights in his side mirror.

Caution welled inside of him as the black sedan crept past his location, braking every so often, before driving forward again. The same black car with Montana plates he'd seen a week ago on Main Street, the day of the purse-snatching ruse.

Nick picked up the notepad he kept on the seat in the truck and jotted down the license-plate number. If he'd doubted it before, he didn't doubt it anymore.

Grace Marshall was being followed. And she knew

it, judging by the practiced evasive move he'd just witnessed.

The car coasted past her house without stopping, flipped a U-turn in the cul-de-sac several blocks ahead and came back for a second pass.

Reaching down, Nick flipped on his lights and caught the driver in the face with his high beams. Just before he dimmed them, he got a good look at the man behind the wheel. White male, mid-to-late thirties, dark brown hair. He stored the description in his memory as he turned the key and fired the engine.

He pulled out into the street, headed in the opposite direction. With any luck he'd pick up the sedan's trail once he made the cul-de-sac and came around to the main road. That should put some distance between them to avoid the driver's suspicion.

Nick saw the car's brake lights come on along with his left-turn signal. He was heading back toward Freedom.

A zip of anticipation buzzed over Nick's nerves, reminding him of his glory days as a U.S. Army Ranger. He'd been good at his job, one of the best, until a mistake had cost several of his buddies their lives.

His mistake.

Gripping the wheel until his fingers stung, he braked at the stop sign and watched a single car pass, then he pulled out behind it. The added buffer would assure that his pursuit went undetected.

He loosened his stranglehold on the steering wheel, but the emotions inside of him refused to relent. Sucking in a deep breath, he focused on the taillights of the black sedan, determined to follow it. Out-of-state plates probably meant he'd make a beeline for one of the half a dozen motels scattered along the main artery into Freedom.

Nick's suspicions were confirmed when the sedan's blinker popped on. He braked and took a right into the parking lot of the Sundown Motel.

Nick rolled past just as the man exited the car. Satisfied, he decided to call it a night, and headed for the ranch on the other end of town. Whoever the man was, he'd at least been able to peg the general location of Grace and Caleb's home. Concern adhered to Nick's nerves. Whatever the guy wanted, it couldn't be good.

A sudden and insatiable need to protect Grace and Caleb Marshall welled from deep inside of him.

Half a mile down the road, he turned around. He headed back out to her street, relieved to see the black car still parked in the motel lot as he cruised past.

He could afford to spend the next couple of hours watching over her…just in case the man in the black sedan decided to take another pass. Besides, there wasn't a chance he'd be getting much in the way of sleep tonight anyway. Not with the brutal images from his past now playing inside of his head.

"ROUGH NIGHT, CAVANAUGH?" Nolan asked as he pulled out his chair at the head of the conference table and sat down.

"Monday morning at 0600 hours is always rough, sir," Nick said, trying to blink the grit out of his eyes. Watching over Grace and Caleb was beginning to take its toll, even though Grace Marshall hadn't left her home the entire weekend. Or opened the blinds, or stepped outside for that matter. Conclusion?

Grace Marshall was scared.

"I know this is strictly your assignment, Nick, but we're a team, and if there's any way we can help—"

"I'll let you know." He nodded to Nolan, knowing full well that he meant every word of it. But his assignment for Governor Lockhart was sensitive. The fact that team member Parker McKenna was involved with Bailey Lockhart, the governor's daughter, and would soon become Lila Lockhart's son-in-law, only added to the need for a discreet investigation. The kicker: Grace Marshall worked for Bailey Lockhart, her possible half sister, at Cradles to Crayons.

Nick rubbed his eyes again and took a swallow from his coffee mug as one by one the team members settled at the table.

Amelia brought a couple of thermoses of coffee into the conference room and put them down in the middle of the table before leaving the room and closing the door behind her.

"Sorry about the 0600, but I've got an early flight out to D.C. for the preliminary on Governor Lockhart's December fundraiser there. I'll be gone until Thursday." Nolan trained his attention on Parker McKenna. "I'd like you to run point on the governor's security while I'm gone."

"Sure thing. I've already had our tech beef up the cameras at the ranch, and extended the visual coverage perimeter around the property. We're in good shape."

"Excellent work. We can't relax our vigilance until she's safely back in Austin at the end of the month." Nolan scribbled something on his notepad and turned his attention to Wade Coltrane. "Anything on the contact list from Trevor Lewis's cell phone?"

"He damn sure liked pizza," Wade said. "Called for

takeout twice a week for months. He also called Stacy Giordano on a regular basis. One name did come up half a dozen times in the last month. A Wes Bradley."

"Sound familiar, anyone?" Nolan asked as he scanned the faces of his team members.

Nick mulled the name and he shook his head. "Never heard it before."

"Sheriff Hale is working on a court order to obtain the phone records," Wade said. "Using cell-tower pings to see if Wes Bradley was in the area."

"Great work. Let's run Wes Bradley through the database and see if we get a hit. Lewis wasn't in this alone. Whoever takes the assignment, be sure to get ahold of the information Harlan has on Lewis's connections to the anarchist group who protested at the governor's fundraiser. See if we can make a connection between Bradley and the group, as well."

"I'll take that assignment," Matteo Soarez said as he jotted the information down.

"And I'll volunteer to check out Stacy Giordano." A wide grin spread on Harlan's face as his jest rubbed everyone's humor bone and scrubbed the tension off of the serious conversation for an instant.

"Hell, you've been checking her out since the first time you met her." Nick laughed, watching his buddy's features soften. Harlan McClain was 110 percent in love with Stacy Giordano. And he'd come within a heartbeat of losing her because of Trevor Lewis.

"All right, you guys, knock it off." Nolan chuckled under his breath. "We'll hold another briefing on Friday morning at 0800 hours. Let's make some progress. Governor Lockhart isn't safe until we nail Lewis's accomplice."

Nick's cell phone rang. He pulled it off his belt and stared down at the number, then flipped it open.

"Sheriff Hale. Good morning." He pushed his chair back and stood up, wanting to put some distance between himself and the other team members.

"Good and early," Hale shot back.

Nick relaxed. He liked Bernard Hale. "Better get your coffee on."

Hale snorted. "I ran the plate number you gave me. Came back registered to a Mamie Ashbury in Dillon, Montana. I gave her a phone call and low and behold, the plate belongs on her husband's old pickup. Trouble is, he's been dead for three years, and the truck is parked in their barn. She hustled out there and discovered the front and rear plates are missin'."

"Not anymore. They've turned up on a late-model sedan."

"About that black car, Nick. One of my deputies found it abandoned in a ditch along Highway 83 this mornin'. Ran the plates and found my inquiry. Ran the VIN number, as well, and it came back to an owner in Amarillo, a Mr. Maxwell Brewster. He claims he sold the car through a newspaper ad three weeks ago."

Worry sliced across Nick's nerves like a razor blade. "Can you give me his contact information, Sheriff?"

"Sure."

Nick grabbed his notepad off the conference table. "Go ahead."

Hale rambled off the phone number; Nick wrote it down. "Thanks. I'd like to follow up and get a physical description of the man he sold the car to."

"No problem, son. Good luck. Let me know if you need any more assistance."

"Thanks, Bernard." Nick closed his phone and turned back to an empty conference room. He tossed the pad onto the table and rested both of his palms on the edge. One step forward, three steps back. At least he'd been able to make the car tailing Grace Marshall. Now he'd have no way of knowing if the guy was still following her until he spotted his new wheels. If he was able to spot them. The guy was cunning. He'd left a dead end when he dumped the black sedan. Hell, Nick would even bet the interior of the car had been wiped clean of any fingerprints.

"Nick?" Amelia stood in the doorway of the conference room.

"Yes." He looked up.

"There's someone here to see you. Shall I show them in here?"

Nick straightened. "Sure."

Amelia disappeared as he shuffled his paperwork into the file on the table. Who would visit him at CSaI headquarters? Most of his work was accomplished in the field, without the trappings of a storefront that could overexpose the CSaI team. He'd only given out a couple of business cards with the information on them since he'd become a part of the group....

His muscles tensed between his shoulder blades as he stepped around the table, listening to Amelia's voice in the outer office as it amplified.

"Right this way, Miss...?"

"Marshall. Grace Marshall."

Nick braced himself for another face-to-face with the unsuspecting focus of his investigation for Governor Lockhart. Rarely did a mark come to him, and a measure of curiosity zipped across his nerves.

Did she know he'd been watching her home this weekend? Had she made him and believed he was some sort of crazy stalker? Was she here to tell him to flake off, or that she planned to call the cops?

Every scenario he could use to justify her visit vanished from his mind as she stepped into the conference room.

She looked beautiful this morning with her long hair let loose in sexy blond strands, her tentative blue-eyed gaze locking with his.

He was in some serious trouble.

"I'll let you two speak in private." Amelia stepped out and pulled the door closed.

"I'm sorry to just show up like this," Grace said as she fingered his business card in her left hand. "But I desperately need your help."

Chapter Four

A wave of concern washed over him. He shrugged it off as he reached out to take her hand.

"I'm not sure what I can do for you, Grace." Their palms touched and he closed his fingers around hers. Her grip was firm, her hand delicate but strong. An instant surge of protectiveness consumed him. He released her hand and stepped back. "Have a seat."

"Thank you." Grace eased herself into a chair at the massive table, thankful that her legs hadn't collapsed from underneath her the moment she entered the room. Every wall she'd erected to protect herself and Caleb was being compromised by her own hand at this moment, but she had no choice. She couldn't let her son die because she was afraid to reach out when she needed help, and Nick Cavanaugh was the first man she'd met in Freedom who gave her a sense of hope.

He sat down at the table across from her. She was grateful for the distance that separated her from the handsome man who now studied her with eyes that seemed to calculate every aspect of her. It didn't help, either, that she could smell the lingering scent of his clean aftershave in the room.

"I don't normally do things like this, but as I told

you in the hospital parking lot, my son, Caleb, needs a bone-marrow transplant. I'm desperate to find a donor, Mr. Cavanaugh."

Leaning forward, he put his arms on the table and said, "Please, call me Nick."

She nodded, trying to force down a lump that formed in her throat. She tried not to stare at him, at the hunger in his clear blue eyes, or the strength in his powerful body. He made her feel safe simply by being close to her.

"He won't make it to his fifth birthday if he doesn't receive a transplant soon. He has an added complication—he's AB negative."

"So his blood type isn't easily matched?"

"Yes. It's not impossible to find a matching donor, but it's not that simple. Their HLA, or human leukocyte antigens, need to match on lots of points, as well, or his body will reject the stem cells, but the odds of it happening before…" She couldn't finish the sentence. Couldn't deal with the prospect of living without her little boy. "I was given up for adoption as an infant. And even though I'm not a donor match for Caleb, my birth mother could be. There's a high probability that she has the same rare blood type as him, and their HLA profile will match up. I managed to trace her to Freedom two years ago. She could save his life. That is, if I can find her."

She watched his facial features soften for the first time since she'd entered the room. One unguarded moment from the man of steel sitting across from her was better than none at all.

"The only problem is, I don't know who she is. That's what I need you to find out for me." Grace dug into her purse where she'd placed it in her lap. "I have a redacted copy of the adoption paperwork signed by the judge. That's how I traced her to Freedom. But other than a Jane Doe of a designated age, I don't have much else." She pulled out the copy and slid it across the table toward him. "I can pay you a small retainer."

Nick's gut cinched in a knot he wasn't sure he'd ever get untied. He should have seen this coming, known how to react, like a soldier on a mission. Duty. But he was sitting across the table from a woman with a dying child. It didn't get more real than that. Had his years on the battlefield turned him into a heartless monster?

"Please help me find her." The plea in her voice cut like a knife.

Slowly he nodded, unsure whether voluntarily or involuntarily; he only knew it felt good in his soul to take up on the side of honor. "I'll see what I can come up with." He picked up the adoption paperwork and flipped it over. "Where can I contact you?"

A shallow smile pulled at her mouth and he found his thoughts wandering to her lips for an instant.

She rattled off her cell number. "I work at Cradles to Crayons most mornings, so you could leave me a message there, and starting next Monday, I'll be working a couple nights a week at Talk of the Town Café if you'd like to speak to me in person."

Nick wrote down her number, new information to him, but he already knew her work schedule at the preschool.

"You're going to go to work for Faith Scott?"

"Yes." Grace put her purse on the table, pushed back her chair and stood up. "I don't know how to thank you enough, Nick."

Staring across at her, he could see the relief in her eyes.

"Just tell Caleb to hang in there, would you?"

"I will." She picked up her purse and without a backward glance, opened the door and left the conference room.

Dammit. What had he done? He rocked back in his chair and closed his eyes. This was one ambush he'd willfully landed himself in. Just like the firefight his bogus intel had drawn his buddies into in Iraq. There were lives at stake.

Frustration ignited a powder keg of guilt inside of him. He had to get it right this time.

Caleb Marshall's life now rested in his hands.

NICK TRIED TO GET COMFORTABLE in one of the oversize leather wingback chairs clustered in the long gallery leading to Governor Lila Lockhart's office, but it was useless. His body was simply reacting to the agitated state of his thoughts.

Succumbing to frustration, he stood up and took to pacing back and forth as he fingered the DNA analysis report in his hand.

The firm sound of his boot soles on the gleaming white marble floor echoed throughout the gallery, but he didn't stop.

He'd gotten himself involved in a conflict of interest that had the potential to blow up in his face, but he brought the image of little Caleb Marshall into his mind's eye and felt his nerves relax.

The little guy deserved a fighting chance, and if this meeting with the governor afforded Caleb that, then he would take whatever fallout it generated around his position at CSaI.

Glancing up he spotted Parker McKenna as he stepped through the double doors at the end of the corridor and strode toward him with a frown on his face.

"Sorry to keep you waiting, buddy, but the shooting attempt still has Lila rattled, and we picked up some movement around the perimeter of the grounds late last night on the security cameras. I put the place in lockdown while Matteo and Harlan checked it out."

"Not a problem." He fell in step next to Parker as he turned and headed back toward the governor's office doors. "Did you find anything in your sweep?"

"A couple of boot tracks in the mud on the northeast corner of the grounds. No one trespassed beyond that point. We cast them for analysis. Matt is taking apart the surveillance video frame by frame, hoping to get a possible ID on the intruder."

"Could be whoever it was, was testing your preparedness, checking to see if you've beefed up the protection around Governor Lockhart. Could be they're scouting for weaknesses in your defenses so they can make another attempt."

Parker stopped outside the doors. "Thanks for your input, Nick. I certainly wish you were involved in this investigation, but I understand you're working on something else for the governor."

"Let me know if I can help with reconnaissance if you get a usable image off the video footage."

"I will." Parker reached down and turned the knob on the right side door, then pushed it open.

Nick stepped inside and listened to the soft click of the latch behind him.

Governor Lila Lockhart looked up from her position behind the massive desk that dominated the antique-filled room. The place had once been her father's safe haven. He only knew it for fact because team member Wade Coltrane had told him this was the place where Lila's father had cut a land deal to help out a desperate Henry Kemp. A deal that had left the Lockharts rich and the Kemps struggling to hold on to the remainder of their ranch.

"Agent Cavanaugh. Please, come in. I'm anxious to hear about your progress on the matter we discussed."

Nick encased his intentions in armor and walked to the desk, where he shook Lila's outstretched hand.

"I don't have to tell you how sensitive this matter is."

"No."

"Good. Have a seat and tell me, were you able to get any information based on the license-plate number I saw the morning the family picked up the infant?" She stared at him with an unemotional intensity that spoke of analytical precision, but somewhere under her polished exterior she had to have an emotional response of some kind. That infant had been her child, her own flesh and blood.

He shrugged it off and lowered himself into one of the two chairs in front of the desk. "I was able to trace the old plate number you gave me to a Claudine and Ralph Wilson in Amarillo. They're both deceased now. A car accident four years ago."

For an instant Lila's facade melted and her blue eyes took on a watery sheen that she easily blinked away. "And what of the child? Were you able to make a DNA match between us?"

"Yes. She's your daughter. She's alive, well and living here in Freedom."

Lila sucked in a quick breath and leaned back in her chair. "Does she know I'm her birth mother and that I gave her up for adoption?"

"No, but she's here with the specific task of finding you."

"She must never learn of my identity, and I do not want to know hers. It could jeopardize my bid for the presidency and decimate my political career. The press and my pundits would have a field day with the information. Not even my press secretary would be able to spin the rhetoric before it destroyed me."

"There's more to it, Governor. She has a sick child who needs a bone-marrow transplant. She needs a close blood relative as a donor. She's a mother, and she's desperate."

The color leaked from the governor's face, then returned under her makeup in the form of rosy blotches on her cheeks. "So you believe she could be here to blackmail me into becoming the child's donor, if she's able to discover who I am, or she'll torpedo my presidential aspirations with the scandal it could ignite?"

Nick gritted his teeth. He'd been retained to make sure that scenario never took shape. "I'm monitoring her on a daily basis. She hasn't discovered your identity. She's been working from a redacted copy of the adoption order—that's how she tracked you to Freedom—but you might consider beating her to the punch by becoming an anonymous donor for her child."

"I will not!" Lila's eyes narrowed as she studied him. "Find out how much it's going to cost me to keep her quiet. Better yet, I'll pay out-of-pocket for a Texas statewide bone-marrow drive in Amarillo. Perhaps a donor can be found there."

Tension walked across the back of his neck. He found another focal point in the room, a set of longhorns protruding from a velvet-covered mounting. The governor's callous response was wreaking havoc on his sense of right, but he hadn't been handed this assignment so he could advocate for Grace on the other side. He'd been hired to make sure none of it ever came to light.

"A lot of desperate recipients could benefit from that, Governor. Maybe even your own grandson."

"I'll put the wheels in motion." She nodded, showing no sign that the word *grandson* had even penetrated her seemingly glacial emotions.

"Assure me you'll continue to monitor the situation, keep her quiet and keep me informed?"

"You have my word." Nick gritted his teeth and stood up. Maybe the bone-marrow drive would produce a donor for Caleb. He had to hang hope on that.

"Bart speaks highly of you, Agent Cavanaugh. That's why I chose you to take this assignment. Don't let me down."

He nodded to the governor and she went back to work on the papers scattered across the desktop in front of her.

Nick went to the door. He grasped the knob, turned it and stepped out into the corridor, spotting Parker McKenna coming toward him at a fast clip.

"Nick. I need you in the control room. Matt has isolated a couple frames of last night's intruder. He'd like you to take a look. Says the guy looks familiar."

Pulling the door closed behind him, he fell in step next to Parker.

"Let me guess. The thug from the hospital?"

"He says it could be, but he wants you to take a look, as well. Back up his call."

Caution worked its way through him. It made sense that the guy who'd made sure Trevor Lewis never spoke again was the one who'd tried their defenses at the ranch. Could he be the shooter, as well?

Nick followed Parker down a narrow hallway off of the gallery. A sharp right and they were standing in a small room with a bank of security-camera feeds lining the wall.

Matteo glanced up at him. "I think it's him, Nick." He pushed and held a button and Nick watched the image click backward, before pausing for an instant. He moved closer, leaned in and studied the fuzzy picture on the monitor.

"We captured a few seconds of physical movement before he faded out of camera range." Matt pushed the pause button again and set the figure in motion.

Nick watched the ski-mask-clad intruder stand up from a crouching position, turn and move out of sight. "Same powerful build. Approximately the same height. I'd say he's the man who took Lewis out. Could be our shooter, as well. Maybe you should contact the deputy whose uniform he took. They'd have to be about the same size. Maybe he'll remember something if you show him the footage."

"Good call. We'll get on it." Parker headed out of the control room, presumably to contact the deputy the thug had almost killed with a violent blow to the head.

Matt paused the video and turned his chair. "What's up?"

Nick crossed his arms over his chest and leaned against the doorjamb. "I need a favor."

"If it involves stealing more glasses from Talk of the Town you can count me out. Faith is protective of those damn glasses."

"She told you, huh?"

"She mentioned you pocketed one and promised to bring it back washed."

A smile busted loose and spread on his face. "It's at headquarters. I'll see that it makes the trip back to the café. But that's not the favor I need."

"I was afraid you'd say that." The grin on Matt's face confirmed that his buddy was all in.

"Faith just hired a woman to work some evenings at the café, a Grace Marshall."

"I've met her. She's gorgeous, and nice. We like her."

"I need to see the employment application she filled out."

"Damn." Matteo stood up and pushed in the chair. "I'm not sure I wanna go there, Nick."

"I need to know who her previous employer was, or her previous address before she moved to Freedom. I know she grew up in Amarillo, but after college in Texas, she married and disappeared. I've got a hole to plug in her background, or at least I've got to know what fits in it."

"Does this involve your special assignment for Governor Lockhart?"

"Yeah." In a roundabout way it had everything to do with his assignment, but deep down he needed to get a handle on who was following Grace and why she was running scared. Besides, he was responsible for keeping her under surveillance and that meant keeping her and Caleb safe.

"I'll see what I can do."

"Thanks, man." Nick pushed away from the door and followed Matteo out of the control room. "I owe you one."

"Just bring Faith's glass back…clean."

They parted company in the gallery and Nick slipped out the front door of Governor Lockhart's mansion.

At least two positive things had come out of the past hour; he was still grappling with the negatives. But number one, he was duty-bound to protect Grace and Caleb Marshall while he made sure Grace never learned she was the illegitimate daughter of Governor Lila Lockhart. Number two, he planned to parlay the governor's promise of a donor drive by becoming the first to be tested. It should cost her a cool million, or two, and work to soothe his bruised sense of honor, but could it save Caleb's life?

Nick climbed into his pickup, fired the engine and rolled out of the drive, headed for Holy Cross Hospital.

SORE BUT SATISFIED, Nick stepped out of the elevator on the ground floor of Holy Cross Hospital and headed for the exit, thinking about Caleb Marshall. The doctors had taken a sample of his bone marrow and would test to see if he was a match for Grace's son. The little guy had no doubt endured the painful procedure he'd just experienced, dozens of times.

Respect and admiration bubbled up inside of him. Caleb Marshall was a fighter.

His cell phone vibrated in his shirt pocket.

Nick fingered it open and stared at the number on the screen. Anticipation glided over his nerves.

"Grace?"

"I'm sorry to bother you, Nick, but there's been some

trouble at my condo and I'm afraid to go inside alone. Caleb and I are still in the car. Can you come?"

"I'll be right there. Where do you live?" His worry level notched up as he hurried to his pickup.

He already knew her address, but he couldn't risk exposure by showing up without having the information come from her first. She rattled off the location, her voice hedged with fear that came out in her wavering pitch.

"That's five minutes from my location. Hang on." He closed his phone, jumped in his truck and took off.

Chapter Five

Grace stared at the closed garage door from across the street as another chill assaulted her body. This was the point where she threw whatever she could carry into a suitcase and skipped town.

He'd found her again.

Adjusting her rearview mirror, she looked at Caleb where he sat strapped in his car seat sound asleep.

Tears welled in her eyes as she studied her tiny son. He was extremely pale today. Not even his normally rosy-hued, chubby cheeks showed signs of color.

She couldn't run. Not this time, not when she was so close to the woman who could save his life. She may never get another chance to get it right. She wiped her eyes and thought about Nick Cavanaugh. There had never been someone she could turn to before him. She'd been on her own since she'd decided to disappear.

Reaching up, she eased the mirror back into place, and jumped. The grill of a pickup filled the rearview. In a panic she hit the auto-locks again just to be certain, but relaxed when movement in her peripheral vision materialized in the form of Nick Cavanaugh standing next to her car.

Grace turned the key and rolled down the driver-side window. "Thank God you're here."

He squatted down on the curb next to her car, reached inside the open window and put his hand on her shoulder. "Are you and Caleb all right?"

Heat scorched her skin under his touch. She leaned into it for an instant before he withdrew his hand. "We're fine, but when I opened the garage to pull in…I knew he'd been here. He could still be inside. I didn't feel safe taking Caleb in without knowing for certain, so I closed the overhead door and parked over here to wait." Tension vibrated across her nerves. She knew what his next question would be even before he asked it.

"Did you call the police?"

"No. I called you." She stared at him, trying to gauge his response to the tiny amount of information she'd given him. She knew he would require more. So much more. Maybe more than she could give.

"I know that's lame, but I'll tell you everything another time. Suffice to say, I've got a stalker."

Awareness wove a path through him as he contemplated her situation. A stalker would explain the man in the black sedan, but not why she hadn't called the police.

He glanced at Caleb asleep in the backseat and his insides went to mush. "Do you lock the entry door from the garage into the house?"

"Always." She pulled her keys out of the ignition, spun the key off the metal ring and handed it to him.

Nick took it and shoved it into his shirt pocket. "Sit tight, lock your doors. I'll check it out. Wait for my all clear." He reached back with his right hand and adjusted the weapons holster he'd clipped onto his belt before he got out of his pickup.

"Open the garage." He stood up, listening to the grind of the overhead door as it responded to the remote opener she'd activated from inside of her car. "Close it the second I'm inside. Do you understand?" He didn't wait for a response to the request. Most people wanted all escape routes left open for them; he wanted the opposite, to trap the intruder inside if he could.

He took off across the street, focused on the condo, locked in stealth mode, but he wasn't prepared for what he saw as he slipped inside the garage and pulled his 9 mm.

Spray painted the entire length of the back wall in running bloodred letters was the word *MURDERER.*

Nick blended into the corner next to the entrance and raised his weapon as the garage-door opener came to life and the door began its slow descent.

A security light came on, soaking the interior in low light.

Whoever Grace's stalker was, he'd made damn sure those letters were the first thing she saw. His effort smacked of some sick psychological need to mentally harass her. Nick's caution level elevated.

The door touched down on the concrete floor. The mechanical hum of the opener ceased.

Nick listened for sounds of movement inside the condo. Nothing. Was he gone? Or hiding inside, waiting to strike?

There was only one way to find out.

He pushed away from the wall and moved to the door leading into the house without making a sound. If the

thug was still here, he knew the opener had been triggered.

Pausing next to the threshold, he glanced at the knob.
He wasn't going to need a key to get in, and neither
was Grace. The thing had been pried open between the
kick-plate and the jamb, judging by the fresh tool marks
gouged into the wooden casing.

Pistol aimed, Nick pushed the door open using the
edge of the jamb for cover. Utility room. Clear.

Stepping inside, he scanned the small cubicle for
hiding places, then turned his focus on the kitchen dead
ahead. Inching out into the room, he prepared to take
out the intruder.

Nothing. Only the sound of his heart thundering
inside of his chest.

To the left was a living room, sparsely furnished.
Devoid of pictures or personality. Clear.

Opposite the kitchen was a hallway.

Nick attached himself to the wall and shot a glance
down the narrow corridor. Clear.

Three entrances, probably two bedrooms and a bath.

He cleared the bathroom, jerked open the shower
curtain, then moved down the hall, where he came to
Caleb's room first. He cleared it, noting the neatly made
bed and the stack of books on the nightstand.

On the opposite side of the hallway, a door stood
slightly ajar. It had to be Grace's bedroom.

The hair on the back of his neck stood up.

Stepping across the hall, he took up a tactical position
next to the entrance and pushed the door open.

The smell in the air hit him first: acrid and laced with
a tinge of sulfur.

Gun raised, he cleared the bedroom, then stepped inside for a closer look.

He knew the scent, knew its source. Battery acid. Grace's bedroom was drenched in it, from across her neatly made bed, to the dresser in the corner. The chemical had already stopped eating away at everything it had touched and had turned to flaky white powder.

He pulled in a breath and holstered his weapon, aware that nothing personal was in plain sight—no pictures, no mementos, nothing. Her bedroom could be at the local motel and have more personality than this room had. Curious, he stepped to the closet and slid it open, ready to take on anything that popped out, but he found himself staring at a large suitcase and four or five outfits hanging on the bar inside.

Three pairs of shoes were neatly placed on the floor. The upper shelf was bare.

Stepping back, he took one last look, his gaze lingering on her bed for longer than felt comfortable. He was duty-bound to keep her safe.

Nick left the room, closing the door behind him. He headed for the front entry to give Grace the all-clear sign. He hadn't surprised an intruder, but he had discovered a few things about Grace Marshall. She was living lean. He'd seen the tactic in Iraq on his recon missions. The enemy always traveled light. They could clear out in a matter of minutes and fade into the twilight to fight another day. But he didn't plan on letting that happen, not this time.

His stomach fisted as he unlocked the front door, stepped outside and waved to Grace, who started her car and pulled into the driveway in front of the garage door.

Nick hurried down the sidewalk to meet her, glad

she hadn't pulled inside. Caleb didn't need to see the ugliness scrawled on the wall, and he hoped for his sake that the little guy had been asleep when they first got home.

"Let me take him," Nick offered as she gently got Caleb out of his car seat and pulled him into her arms.

"Thank you." She handed him off and closed the car door.

"Treatment day?" he asked as he turned and aimed for the front door with Grace next to him. Caleb felt so fragile in his arms, small and vulnerable. A surge of protectiveness flooded his veins and didn't relent.

"Yes. This morning, but he's been like this for the entire afternoon."

Worry washed over Nick's emotions as Grace opened the front door for him and they went inside. "I'll put him in his bed."

She nodded. "I'll change my clothes and make us some coffee."

Nick stopped in his tracks and turned to face her. "You don't want to go into your bedroom right now."

Her eyes widened for an instant. "He was in my bedroom?"

"Yeah. Make that coffee. We need to talk." He walked down the hallway and into Caleb's room, where he gently pulled back the covers and put him down on his bed. He tucked them up around the little boy and stepped back, his heart in a knot he'd never untangle.

Caleb Marshall was dying.

Reality slammed into him with the force of a sledgehammer. In that instant he realized he'd be willing to give up everything he had to ensure Caleb survived.

"Do you have children, Nick?"

Caught off guard, he tensed at the sound of Grace's voice behind him. He pulled himself together, straightened and turned to stare at her. She was leaning against the doorjamb, watching him with those gorgeous shade-of-heaven eyes, slowly taking him prisoner with every glance.

"No," he said, just above a whisper, willing the emotion from his voice. "But I'd like to."

She swallowed hard, her eyes tearing at the edges before she turned away. "Coffee's ready."

"Grace?" He pulled the door to Caleb's room closed and trailed her out into the hallway then into the kitchen where she abruptly stopped with her back to him. From the slight up and down movement of her shoulders, he could tell she was crying.

"Grace." Stepping up next to her, he pressed his hand against her back. He knew she was in emotional pain, knew the raging tangle of emotions assaulting her were winning the battle at the moment.

Without coaxing, she turned into him.

He held her close, feeling an explosion of attraction as he wrapped his arms around her slender shoulders and cupped her head with his hand.

Time stood still. He closed his eyes, feeling the sensation of her against his chest. Hot streaks of desire skittered over his nerve endings. Grace needed to commiserate, not be seduced.

Nick gritted his teeth against the onslaught, and with every measure of restraint he could muster, he released her. "He's going to make it, Grace. He's going to get a transplant." Reaching out he brushed a wayward tear off her cheek with his fingers.

She stared up at him. "You don't understand. I can't

stay in Freedom now that he knows where I live. And I can't leave, or I risk Caleb's only chance for survival."

He grasped her upper arms, desperate to discourage her from running like he was certain she'd done before.

"You don't have to leave Freedom, but you can't stay here. This guy is a nut job. He doused your bedroom with battery acid. Rage like that could escalate into violence, and he'll be back, but I won't let him hurt you or Caleb. We'll contact Sheriff Hale."

She sucked in a quick breath, her eyes filling with tears again as she glanced away. He felt her body tense under his palms.

"No. No cops."

"I want to help you, but you have to tell me what the hell's going on."

Grace's heart threatened to pound out of her chest. She couldn't tell him the truth. Nick Cavanaugh was an honorable man, she knew it, felt it, and the truth could drive him away just when she needed him the most.

"My stalker is a cop with a thick blue line around him." His features softened and she felt the tension in his hold relax as he pulled her to him. She went willingly, turned her head and settled her ear against his chest, listening to the reassuring thud of his heart under her ear. She closed her eyes, trying to remember the last time she'd felt this safe this close to a man, but the past four years of her life were a blur.

"Grace, listen to me."

Pushing back, she looked up at him, concerned by the worry in his voice.

"I want you to pack your things and pull your car into the garage."

She opened her mouth to speak, but he pressed a finger to her lips.

"I'm getting you both out of here," he whispered. "We're a go at dark."

NICK GLANCED IN THE REARVIEW mirror at the headlights several car-lengths back. They'd picked up the tail just after they'd pulled onto the main highway from Grace's condo, even though she'd managed to slip down as low in the seat as she could.

Caleb's car seat was strapped in between them, but he could barely see over the dash. If it was Grace's stalker, he had to have X-ray vision, because Nick had used every diversionary tactic available to make sure they weren't followed. He'd even insisted on pulling into the garage to load up their belongings away from spying eyes. Still, he'd probably been made the moment he answered Grace's call and came roaring down the street like a bat out of Sunday school.

"We've got company."

"He's behind us? Already?" Grace turned and glanced out the rear window for an instant.

"Could be. The vehicle eased in behind us shortly after we left your condo."

"Mister Nick. Where are we going?"

"To my place, buddy."

"Is that where the bays are?"

He chuckled. "Yeah. I'll show them to you in the morning when it's light outside."

"Okay." Caleb bounced his feet back and forth on the edge of the seat and tried to see over the dash of the pickup, but he wasn't tall enough. "I'm high up in the air."

Looking sideways he saw Grace smile in the illumination coming from his dash lights. Life's small talk was pretty simple for a four-year-old, at least for most of them, and their mommas, too. But not for Grace, not right now.

Nick sobered and checked his mirror again. "I need to lose this guy. I don't want to lead him to the ranch."

"Ranch, ranch, ranch, ranch, ranch." Caleb repeated the word, keeping time to the beat with his feet bouncing against the edge of the seat.

"Hey, buddy. I think your transfusion is kickin' in."

"You have no idea," Grace said before she busted out laughing.

It sounded good in his ears. He hoped he would hear it more often once they were safe.

Nick stepped on the gas and watched the speedometer needle climb.

The car tailing them sped up, gaining a car length.

"There's no doubt. He's following us." Nick glanced at Grace for an instant.

"You can't let him catch us."

"Don't worry, sweetheart. I know where Sheriff Hale likes to set his speed traps."

Her eyes went wide, and he guessed that she was considering her aversion to anything that involved the police, including a speeding ticket. "Relax, Grace. They're not all bad."

Nick let off the gas pedal slightly, just enough to reel in the driver behind him. At Freedom's truck route bypass, he took the sweeping turn that would shoot them out onto the highway on the west side of town.

"Faster…faster…faster," Caleb said in an excited voice. "Step on it, Mister Nick!"

Grinning in the dark, Nick pushed the accelerator to the floor as they merged onto the empty highway with the thug on their tail. "How's that, buddy?"

"Faster."

"Caleb," Grace scolded, before she shushed him.

The road dipped in elevation, then hit a rise, dipped again and crested, blasting them right past a police car parked in an unmarked turnout.

Three seconds later the thug behind them passed the patrol car. Two seconds later the lights and siren came on and the officer tore out of his parking spot onto the highway.

"Got you, you bast—" Nick clamped his mouth shut, aware of the tiny pair of ears right next to him.

"Grace, back me up. Get the make on his car when he breezes past. A plate number, too, if you can."

"Okay."

Up ahead he spotted a pull-off and flipped on his right-hand-turn signal, then applied the brakes, bringing the pickup's speed down before he angled in off of the road and watched the thug blow past without touching his brakes.

Grace let out an audible gasp. "A Chevy, something. White. Plate number B485."

"That's what I got, too."

"That was amazing. How did you do that?" Grace asked.

"Nobody likes to endure a traffic stop. Especially not a rogue cop who already believes he's above the law. And I listen to my police scanner."

Chapter Six

Grace fingered the warning ticket Nick had casually tossed on the kitchen counter the night before, then moved to the sink to rinse off the breakfast dishes and put them into the dishwasher.

"I'm going to see the bays," Caleb said from his seat at the bar in the center of the kitchen, where he sat next to Nick. "Mister Nick is going to take me."

"Not without a jacket. It's chilly this morning." Grace turned on the water to scour the plates, cups and silverware. She shut off the faucet, dried her hands on the dish towel hanging next to the sink, then turned to look at the two of them conspiring together at the breakfast bar.

"Your fleece hoodie is in the suitcase, Caleb. It's lying open at the foot of the bed in Mommy's room. Go get it."

"All right." He climbed down off the high stool with help from Nick and took off at a run.

Grace's heart squeezed in her chest. She forced a lump of emotion down and moved to the edge of the counter directly across from him, as she listened to Caleb's hurried footfalls against the hardwood floor in the hallway. "I can't tell you how much I appreciate what you're doing for us."

He stared back at her, a sexy grin bowing his lips. She was struck by his good looks, his physical persona and the intensity of his gaze. Pulse skipping, palms slicking, she dropped her perusal.

"This big, empty house could stand to see some action."

"You picked the right child to make that happen." Feeling the need to qualify her son's ever-changing energy levels, she continued, knowing it was a reality not everyone understood, or could handle on a daily basis for that matter. "That is, whenever he's running on a fresh blood supply. He goes from listless and sleepy to a bundle of energy in a matter of hours. That's why I generally take the sick day my boss, Bailey Lockhart, gives me the morning after he has had a transfusion."

Nick's smile faded. "He's a great kid, Grace. Pepped up or asleep." He slid his hand across the counter to cover hers. It took every ounce of restraint she possessed not to fall apart that instant. She couldn't remain here forever.

"I want you and Caleb to stay for as long as it takes."

She stared at him, feeling the heat in his touch as it pulsed along her arm in an intimate connection she could feel growing between them.

"I'll find a way to neutralize the creep stalking you." There was absolute seriousness in the set of his mouth and the slight narrowing of his intense blue eyes.

A blade of fear knifed through her. "Be careful, Nick. He's got friends with badges who don't seem to mind helping him. He's been able to trace me everywhere I've been for the last three years."

"That's when you run?"

"Yes."

"Who is he, Grace?"

Her emotions locked up, strangled with tension that wound tight like a cord inside of her. The whole truth could drive Nick away when she needed his help the most, but she couldn't live with herself if she let him walk into a trap because he hadn't been forewarned.

"His name's Rodney Marshall. He's my ex-brother-in-law."

"Your ex-husband's brother?"

"My dead husband's brother."

Nick didn't flinch, didn't follow her statement up by questioning why or how—much to her relief. Instead he squeezed her hand before he pulled back.

"You haven't seen the brotherhood I hang out with. They're exes, too. Ex-military." He smiled again, making her fears recede, but only a fraction.

Rodney Marshall was dangerous, especially high on the poison of a grudge. A vendetta against her for what she'd done to...

The sound of Caleb's footfalls were obscured in a rhythmical scraping noise that came with him into the kitchen.

She turned to look at him where he stood grinning, wearing a pair of Nick's cowboy boots, whose leather shafts ended just above his kneecaps, and a cowboy hat he unceremoniously pushed back with his hand to look up at them, but no jacket.

"Caleb. We're guests here. You can't get into Mister Nick's things without permission."

Turning her attention on Nick she realized he was laughing under his breath so hard he almost fell off his stool as he stared down at Caleb. "Looks like we need to make some adjustments, buddy."

He looked over at her, his handsome face contorted with amusement, and she was relieved he wasn't upset with Caleb for poking around in his things.

"I'll go find his jacket."

"What's your bay's name?" Caleb asked Nick as she left the kitchen, headed down the hallway to her room in search of the fleece hoodie. "Saddle him up. I wanna ride."

She smiled as she entered the spacious room Nick had put her and Caleb in last night, thinking of the influence Zachary Giordano's Wild West horse tales, recited at recess at Cradles to Crayons, had had on Caleb's desire to be a cowboy someday.

Sucking in a breath, she paused next to the empty suitcase and stared at the pile of clothing her son had torn through in his excitement to get outside to see Nick's horses.

Going to her knees, she scrounged until she found the jacket at the bottom of the stack. Living out of a suitcase had some advantages, but for the life of her she couldn't think of a single one right now.

Shaking out the fleece hoodie, she headed for the kitchen, unable to hear the sound of their voices.

Once she reached the room she knew why. The place was empty.

Concerned, she headed for the big window above the sink and looked out into the backyard, spotting Nick and Caleb walking across the grass at a turtle's pace, with Caleb's oversize cowboy garb slowing them down. He was wearing one of Nick's sweatshirts with the sleeves rolled up, and the tails of a dish towel hung out from under the cowboy hat, where Nick had used it to fill up the space between the brim and Caleb's head.

At least he could see where he was going.

They stopped to talk for a moment, before Nick scooped him up and planted him atop his shoulders.

An ache squeezed inside of her. She pressed her hand to her chest to protect her heart. Being alone was hard; she'd learned to live with it, but seeing her son looking up at Nick Cavanaugh put it all into painful perspective for her.

Caleb was alone, too, deprived of a strong male role model. Running away again would only make that harder than ever to remedy.

She had to stay.

"WHAT THE HELL?" he mouthed under his breath, adjusting the focus on his binoculars. He was on his belly on the ground three hundred yards east of the horse corral.

He didn't move, didn't breathe, didn't flinch as Agent Cavanaugh lifted a funnily dressed little kid off his shoulders, put him down and stared in his direction for a moment. He'd never seen the kid before. Maybe Cavanaugh had a nephew?

Cool Texas wind stirred the dry brown grass surrounding him, but he remained perfectly still, like a diamondback waiting to strike, minus any warning rattle.

The agent was generally gone by this time of the morning, so what did the kid have to do with him still being home? A string of mental curses raced around inside his head. He needed to get in, but he'd have to wait. He couldn't risk detection, not when his plans were firming up so neatly.

"Boom," he whispered, watching the agent turn his back to open the corral gate, before he picked up the boy in his arms and went inside, disappearing in the midst of the horses.

He snaked backward, careful to minimize the amount of dust he raised with his movements. Detection could end his days on the lamb, and he was too damn close to reeling in the big one. He couldn't let that happen.

Inching down below the shallow rise, he made the decision to wait it out, and rolled onto his back to stare up at the graying sky overhead.

If Cavanaugh left early enough and took the brat with him, he could get inside the house.

NICK SCANNED THE TERRAIN well beyond the corral. There it was again. That hinky sensation of being watched that always walked across the back of his neck whenever someone's or something's eyes were boring into him. It had saved his butt more than once in Iraq, but nothing moved in the shocks of fall-brown grass except the morning breeze. Satisfied, he turned and unlatched the corral gate, then picked Caleb up and waded into the cluster of horses.

Caleb's arms quickly locked around his neck.

He felt him tremble as he eyed the horses, whose ears rotated forward as they stared back in curiosity.

"Relax, bud, I've got ya. They're not going to hurt you."

Caleb's death grip softened, but he still eyed the creatures with suspicion.

"This here's Jericho. He's my ropin' horse. I use him to chase the cows." Nick moved in close to the big bay, reached out and patted the animal's neck. "Go ahead, give him a pet. He's kid gentle."

In a show of trust, Caleb gingerly extended his right

hand and put it on the horse. A slow grin replaced his look of concern as he stroked his hand along Jericho's neck.

"See. What'd I tell ya?"

He nodded. "Him's nice."

"That's right. Would you like to sit on his back?"

Caleb swallowed, his bright blue eyes widening as he looked at the horse, then back at Nick, then back at the horse.

"It's okay. You don't have to if you don't want to."

"Zachary-G does it." He pulled his hand back and began a nervous game of finger play between his right and left digits.

"I'll stay right here next to you, Caleb."

His desire to do what Zachary-G did eventually overruled his nerves. "Saddle him up, Mister Nick."

Nick grinned. "All right, tiger, here you go." He easily lifted Caleb and set him down on Jericho, but he retained a hold on the little boy's leg just in case. With his left hand, he gathered a handful of black mane. "Hang on to this, Caleb." He gestured and watched him squeeze the mane tightly in both hands.

"You can tell Zachary-G you're riding bareback."

Caleb grinned as he sat atop the big horse, and Nick's heart jolted inside his chest. The little guy had overcome his fear like a trooper. A measure of pride affixed itself to his thoughts.

"That's probably enough for today. Next time I'll saddle him up and we'll take off across the field."

"Fast?" Caleb asked, still smiling.

"As fast as you wanna go."

Caleb nodded, released his handful of horse mane and reached out to Nick with both arms.

Struck by the child's level of trust, Nick gathered him off the animal and carried him to the gate. He pushed it open, stepped outside of the corral and lowered Caleb onto his oversize-boot-clad feet. He latched the gate and turned around, catching a flit of movement in a clump of grass fifty feet to the east.

Caution glided through him as he stared, watching for a second telltale sign. Transfixed, he picked out a pair of eyes watching back. The source of his earlier agitation?

"Caleb, look over there," he whispered to the boy. "A coyote. He's watching us from the grass." Nick squatted down, picked up a clod of dirt and chucked it toward the wild animal. It hit the ground five feet in front of the coyote and broke apart, sending tiny pellets of dirt in his direction.

The coyote bolted and took off.

"Did you see him?"

"Yeah," Caleb said, grinning as he squinted into the midmorning sun that was in the process of escaping into the spotty clouds above.

"Let's get you back inside to your mom."

With one last glance in the rangy coyote's direction, Nick and Caleb headed for the house.

PROGRESS TODAY ON HIS IED wasn't happening, he decided. Shortly after Agent Cavanaugh and the kid had gone inside, he'd spotted a woman standing at the kitchen window.

Aggravated with the delay, he made the decision to pack it in and head for the lower twenty acres on the edge of the ranch. He'd been holed up in an abandoned barn for the past month, waiting for his opportunity to strike again—while he intermittently used Agent Cavanaugh's big, empty house with its closed-off rooms as if it were his own.

NICK STARED AT THE PAPERWORK on his desk and rocked back in his chair. Since leaving the ranch around noon, he hadn't been able to get Grace and Caleb Marshall off of his mind, or the fact that the assignment he'd taken from Governor Lockhart could force him to compromise his values. It would be different if Grace were here in Freedom to blackmail the governor, but that thread had come unraveled the moment he met Caleb. Still, there were things about Grace that concerned him. Like why in the hell her ex-brother-in-law was stalking her. Did she renege on giving him her deceased husband's baseball-card collection like he'd been promised in the will? Or not hand back some family heirloom? Doubtful.

"Hey, bro." Matteo pulled a chair up next to his desk and sat down. "You got a pen? I finagled a glance at Grace Marshall's employment application."

Nick straightened in his chair, feeling guilty for asking, but anxious for the information that could help explain Grace's predicament.

"Three years ago, she worked at a preschool in Billings, Montana, called Love and Learn. After that she listed a restaurant in Amarillo called the Armadillo. Nothing here in Freedom except part-time at Cradles to Crayons."

Nick wrote down the information, then opened his bottom desk drawer and pulled out the water glass he'd lifted from Talk of the Town.

"It's clean. Be sure you tell Faith."

Matt took the cup. "I sure hope you know what you're doing. Grace seems like a nice woman."

"She is, and her son, Caleb, is a great kid."

"So what's the problem?"

"No problem. Not one I can elaborate on."

Matt shrugged his shoulders. "Okay, but you know the team is always here."

He nodded. "I appreciate that. How are things at the Twin Harts? Any lead on the guy in the surveillance tape?"

"Nothing but the single boot track we cast. Came back as a standard issue, U.S. Marine Corps."

"Can I see it?"

"Yeah." Matt stood up, went to his desk, picked up the casting and brought it over, where he handed it to Nick.

"Looks like a boot without much wear. Probably never seen a tour of duty. Could be our guy just likes to dress up and play soldier." He handed the cast print back to Matteo.

Amelia walked up and put a piece of paper on Nick's desk. "Your plate number B485 belongs on a 1998 Chevy Impala, white. Registered owner is a Tom McCarthy, lives right here in Freedom. I copied down his phone number for you."

Nick looked up. "Thanks, Amelia."

"You're welcome," she said over her shoulder as she turned and headed back to her desk.

"I swear, she's former CIA," Matt said in a conspiratorial voice loud enough that Nick was certain she'd heard it.

"Efficient and beautiful," he said, watching her turn her head slightly. Anything was possible, Nick decided.

After all, their boss, Bart Bellows, had spent time working for the CIA, or at least that was the clandestine rumor.

"Take it easy. I've got to get home—I'm taking my two favorite girls out to dinner tonight," Matt said, referring to Faith and her baby girl, Kaleigh.

"Have a good time." Nick watched Matt park the chair where he'd found it, grab his jacket and head out. Suddenly Nick realized that he also had someone to go home to this evening for the first time since he'd joined the CSaI and moved to Freedom. But he had a phone call to make before he took off.

He lifted the telephone receiver and dialed the number on the sheet of paper Amelia had given him.

"Hello."

"Tom McCarthy?"

"Yeah."

"My name's Nick. I'd like to inquire about your 1998 white Chevy Impala."

"Sold it. Yesterday, as a matter of fact. Sorry, you're too late. I should have pulled the newspaper ad."

"Sounds like my buddy beat me to it. Was he of medium build, dark brown hair, paid cash, named Rodney Marshall?"

"Yeah. You described him, but he said his name was James Allred. Says he lives in Amarillo."

"Sorry. My mistake." Nick hung up the phone. It would make sense that Rodney had used an alias to buy another car from a private party. He would probably eventually ditch it somewhere just like he'd done with the black sedan. Rodney Marshall was going to be as predictable as the lack of rain in southern Texas. The only thing Nick wanted now was to know what motivated the guy. And only Grace Marshall knew that for sure.

He shuffled together the written request he'd printed out addressed to the attorney general of the state of Texas, asking for a medical waiver to open a sealed adoption file, a request that didn't have a chance of being granted. It was, however, a step that any good investigator would naturally seek first. All he needed was for Grace Marshall to sign the request.

A wave of guilt showered him, pooling in the corners of his mind. He had every intention of confronting Governor Lockhart again as soon as possible, but next time he planned to put a name to the faceless baby the governor had given up. Maybe knowing for sure who her daughter was would change things. Maybe then she would reconsider.

Pushing the paperwork into a clean file folder, he uncovered the facts Matteo had recovered from Grace's employment application for Talk of the Town.

He had her fingerprints. He had the names of the cities where she'd resided in the past three years; Billings, Montana, being the only hole he needed to plug. He needed to run all of her background information to cover his bases, but... Disgusted with himself, he grabbed the paper, opened the top drawer of his desk and shoved it inside.

"I'm calling it an afternoon," Amelia said as she flicked off the lamp on her desk.

"I won't be in the office tomorrow. I'm working on assignment." Nick turned in his desk chair. "I need the gray Tahoe from the company garage in exchange for my pickup. It's a little hot right now."

Amelia chuckled. "I'm not even going to ask, Cavanaugh. The key ring is hanging on the board in the supply room, and don't forget Nolan's roundtable on Friday at 0800. You missed my memo this morning."

"I'm all over it." Nick stood up, pushed his chair in and picked up the file, suddenly anxious to get home.

Chapter Seven

"Go and wash your hands," Grace said to Caleb, watching him drag his feet as he begrudgingly headed down the hallway to the powder room to scrub off a busy day of petting horses, playing with toy cars and getting settled in.

She positioned the silverware on the dining-room table, wondering if she'd overstepped her bounds. This was Nick Cavanaugh's home, they were guests, albeit forced guests, but they all had to eat, and she loved to cook.

The flash of car lights bounced off the closed drapes of the dining-room window for an instant. Grace's heart did a somersault. For some odd reason she felt like a three-year-old on Christmas morning, giddy with anticipation.

She shrugged it off and headed for the front door, anxious to test her skills at disarming the security system. She hadn't ventured outside today, much to Caleb's displeasure, but it wasn't safe until Rodney gave up, or left town, neither of which she was convinced he'd do.

An ounce of caution worked through her as she raised her finger to punch in the code Nick had given her. She hesitated, rocked up onto her tiptoes, put her eye to the peephole and stared out at an unfamiliar vehicle as it rolled to a stop in the circle driveway.

It wasn't Nick's white truck.

"Mommy, I'm clean."

Panic aced out caution in her bloodstream as she turned to look at Caleb. Hide, they needed to hide, until the possible threat passed.

"Come on, honey. Momma needs to wash up, too, then we'll have supper." She scooped Caleb up in her arms and headed for the bedroom, her heart hammering against her rib cage.

She ducked inside the room, closed the door and turned the lock. Heading straight for the attached bathroom, she stepped inside, locked the door and turned off the light. The sensor night-light plugged into the socket next to the sink automatically came on.

"Cool," Caleb said, fidgeting to be put down.

"I'll let you go, Caleb, but you have to promise to play the quiet game with Mommy."

He nodded and grinned, thrilled with the idea of a competition.

"Good boy. No talking for ten minutes," Grace whispered as she let him down, took his tiny hand and led him over to the tub.

The moment she released him, he slapped both hands over his mouth and stared up at her, his big blue eyes crinkling at the corners. Caleb was grinning underneath his palms.

Taken by his innocent gesture, she sat down on the edge of the bathtub, pulled him into her arms and rocked him as she listened to the unfamiliar sounds of the house. If the alarm was triggered, the local police would respond within minutes. According to Nick, it was wired into the station downtown.

Still, she scanned the bathroom for anything she could use as a weapon, finally settling on the heavy metal towel stand sitting on the vanity.

The first shrill whoop of the alarm sent a shiver through her that rippled to her toes.

Caleb's hands went from covering his mouth to covering his ears. Tears welled in his eyes, as his amusement with their game turned to terror at the scary sound.

"It's okay. It's okay," she soothed, the seconds ticking by as she made a decision.

"Mommy's going to make it stop." Grace stood up, turned and sat Caleb in the bathtub. She yanked an oversize towel off the towel bar and cocooned him in it until the only thing showing was his face.

"We're still playing the game. Stay here until I come back for you."

She brushed her hand across the top of his terrycloth-covered head, straightened and pulled the shower curtain shut.

Tension burned through every nerve ending in her body. Reaching out, she locked her hand around the heavy towel stand on the vanity and picked it up.

Fingers trembling, she settled them on the bathroom-door lock, but memories from her past cut a path of hesitation through her resolve. Gritting her teeth, she fought against the need to hide and opened the bathroom door, determined she'd never live in the hell of abuse again. Not from her dead husband. Not from his crazy brother, Rod, or anyone else for that matter.

She sucked in a shaky breath and stepped through the doorway. The bedroom was empty.

Reaching around the edge of the door, she flipped the lock and pulled it closed behind her, hearing it latch with Caleb safely inside.

If Rodney Marshall had finally come to physically exact vengeance on her, then she wasn't going to go down without a fight. She'd bash his head in the first chance she got, or die trying.

THE FRONT-ENTRY DOOR gaped open, Nick's keys still swinging in the keyhole and the file folder on the floor at his feet as he tried to silence the annoying shrill of the security alarm he'd just triggered.

If he hadn't been so focused on seeing Grace and Caleb the moment he got home he would have remembered the confounded thing he'd set this morning.

1-9-3-5 Disarm. He hit Disarm a second time just for good measure. Still the noise echoed throughout the house, setting his nerves on edge. *1-9-3-5 Disarm.* Frustration made his fingers clumsy on the small keypad. He pressed in the code again.

Where was Grace? He smelled the scent of supper in the air. She'd been in the kitchen recently.

A hint of worry shot through him as he abandoned the damn alarm and hurried through the foyer. He took a right and glanced around the empty kitchen and dining room, his stare raking the table, neatly set for three.

"Grace! Caleb!"

His heart rate kicked up.

Pivoting, he rushed to her bedroom door, where he tried the knob.

Locked.

"Grace!" he yelled over the deafening noise. No answer.

Nick raised his booted foot and jammed it into the door.

Wood splintered, the latch let go and the door swung open.

He heard Grace scream, felt the crack of something hard against the back of his skull, then a burst of light and pain.

"Grace." He stumbled forward, catching himself before he hit the floor.

The lights in the room flicked on and he turned slowly to stare at her where she stood to the left of the entrance holding a towel stand.

She dropped it as if it were scalding. It hit the carpet, its thud lost in the blaring sound of the alarm.

Recognition widened her eyes before her features dissolved into horror for the mistake she'd just made.

"Grace." He reached out to her, but rather than step into his arms, she shook her head, took his hand and pulled him out of the room, down the hallway into the foyer where the entry door still stood wide-open.

Reaching down, she pulled his house key out of the keyhole.

The alarm stopped and she pushed the door closed.

In three steps and silence, she was in his arms. "I'm sorry for hitting you," she said as he held her, "but I thought he'd broken in to…"

He felt her tremble. Unnerved by the distress he'd just caused her because he hadn't taken the time to master the logic of the damn security alarm he hardly ever used.

"Are you okay?" he whispered against her hair, pulling in the sweet smell of her, enjoying the feel of her body next to his.

"Better, now that you're here."

"And Caleb?"

"Safe in the bathroom."

"I'm sorry, Grace. I should have called to let you know I'd be driving a different rig tonight."

She leaned back and stared up at him, a serious glint in her incredible blue eyes. "If I'd gotten a look at you coming up the walk before I panicked—"

"No. That's where you're wrong. You responded correctly, took cover and—" he raised his hand to the goose egg swelling on the back of his head "—armed yourself."

"Mommy!"

He released her and they hurried back into the bedroom to get Caleb.

The bathroom knob rattled.

"Caleb? Can you unlock it?" Nick asked, concerned and curious how he'd come through the scare.

The little tiger pulled open the door and rushed out of the bathroom wearing a towel over his head and wrapped around his shoulders. "Mister Nick, you're home!"

Nick scooped him up. "You better believe it." He turned toward Grace, struck by the sweet smile on her lips, lips he wanted to kiss right now. He hustled the wayward thought out of his mind and put Caleb down.

"It smells like your mamma made supper."

"Yeah, cluck-cluck I think. I wanted macaronis."

"Chicken?" He glanced over at Grace, who confirmed her son's word choice.

"Curry Chicken," she said.

"You two head for the table. I'll see if I can get Sheriff Hale turned around before he rolls a patrol unit on the alarm call."

Nick pulled his cell phone off his belt and dialed 9-1-1. As it rang, he followed Grace and Caleb out of the bedroom, stopping in the hallway to give dispatch the information.

Closing his phone, he stood staring after them for a moment. Mother and child. Hand in hand. He was struck by the myriad of emotions that took hold inside of him.

He was driven to protect them. He would always protect them. With his life if necessary.

"THAT WAS SOME KIND OF MAGIC you performed on that freezer-burned cluck-cluck." Nick chuckled as he put the last of the dishes into the sink where Grace was rinsing them off.

"We should probably get to the grocery store," she said, casting him a sideways glance. "Take some of the bachelor out of your pad."

He snorted. "I know I had some other stuff in there. You didn't find any other meat?"

"No. Just a package of chicken breasts and a bag of peas."

Nick opened the dishwasher, feeling at odds with the information. Granted, he ate out at Talk of the Town most nights, then came home to crash, but he remembered loading up at the grocery store just over two weeks ago.

"Don't worry about it, Nick. I'll go shopping after work tomorrow and pick up some things Caleb and I like. Do you have any food aversions?"

"Brussels sprouts." He grinned, glancing out the kitchen window into the darkness for a second.

"Hey, do you see that?" He redrew his focus on a

tiny light, barely visible, a pinprick in the blackness of a moonless night.

Grace squinted. "Yeah. A flashlight maybe. Seems too far away though for us to see if it's a flashlight. Could be a lantern."

Caution glided over him. He stared at the light, trying to isolate its location. "It's down near the abandoned hay barn on the lower twenty acres I don't lease from my boss. There's nothin' down there but rattlers and rabbits."

Grace shuddered. "I hate snakes."

"Relax, they're holed up underground in this cool weather."

"So you lease this ranch?"

"Yeah. It belongs to Bart Bellows, CSaI founder. He built it for his son six years ago, but he was killed in a bombing in Iraq. It's been sitting empty ever since. Bart gave me the option of taking it or an apartment in town. I jumped at the opportunity, took the ranch and drove my horses down from my family's spread in Idaho."

"Under your military camouflage, you're a cowboy." Grace smiled.

"Born and bred." He watched the pinprick of illumination flicker, then dim and go out, leaving only darkness to stare into. "You could be right, Grace. That looked like a lantern being extinguished." He was curious, but not overly concerned with the prospect of having someone trespass on the lower twenty.

He helped Grace finish the dishes and dried his hands on a towel. He'd ride Jericho down there sometime soon to have a look around. One of the neighboring ranchers had probably been in search of a stray cow, or a missing dog.

The patter of Caleb's bare feet in the hallway and out into the kitchen brought Nick around. He leaned against the counter next to Grace, as they both looked down at Caleb dressed in his pajamas.

"Tooth inspection," Grace said.

Caleb opened his mouth wide, then promptly clamped his baby teeth together to show his mother he'd done a good job of brushing.

"Very nice. Now off to bed. You've got preschool in the morning and lots to tell Zachary-G about the horse you sat on today." She reached down and took his hand. "I'll tuck you in."

"I want Mister Nick to tuck me in."

"I'm flattered, buddy, but it's your mamma's call." Nick stared over at Grace, not wanting to tread too deeply into her territory. She was extremely protective of Caleb, and rightly so.

"Do you mind?" she asked, studying him intently. "I need to wipe down the table and counters."

"Are you sure?"

She nodded, a bit too vigorously, let go of Caleb's hand and turned back to the sink, where she picked up the dishcloth and headed for the dining-room table.

"Come on, kiddo." He scooped Caleb up in his arms and headed for the bedroom, concerned about Grace. "We're going to saddle the horses on Saturday and go for a real ride. Next week you'll have a story to tell Zachary-G."

"Okay." Caleb settled against him and laid his head on Nick's shoulder.

In silence, he stepped into the bedroom, went to the bed, pulled back the comforter, lowered the little tiger onto the bed and then tucked him in. "Good night, buddy," he said, reaching out to smooth Caleb's hair with his hand. "I'm glad you're safe here at the ranch. Get some sleep."

Caleb closed his eyes and Nick headed for the door, realizing he could already see the child's energy level dropping.

"Mister Nick," Caleb whispered.

He stopped next to the jamb and turned. "Yeah."

"I like your ranch. Can we go fast on your horse?"

"As fast as you want." He flipped off the light switch next to the door, stepped out into the hallway and gently pulled the door shut, leaving a small opening.

He'd get the damaged latch fixed tomorrow; too bad Caleb's fix wasn't going to be that easy.

Guilt coated his insides as he walked down the hallway and paused in the foyer to stare at the abandoned file folder lying right where he'd dropped it during his attempt to silence the screaming alarm.

The paperwork inside wasn't going to help Caleb. It wasn't going to assure that he survived. Nick raked his hand over his head, walked over and picked it up. Frustrated with the internal battle raging inside of him. *Honor. Duty. Duty. Honor.*

This assignment was suffocating him in an ever-tightening noose. He had to break free soon, or he'd asphyxiate on his own indecision.

"Nick?" The sound of Grace's voice sucked him back from his thoughts. He glanced up to where she stood at the entrance into the kitchen. "Everything okay?"

He tapped the file folder against his palm. "Yeah."

Moving toward her, he saw the gleam of tears in her eyes. Concerned, he brushed his hand against her upper arm.

"I'm sorry, Grace. I shouldn't have taken your night-time ritual. I know how precious he is to you."

"It's not that. I'm grateful you took the time to tuck him in. He needs a strong male role model in his life, Nick. You're all he talked about today, and I'm thrilled. I want Caleb to know there are other men in the world besides the ones he sees at the hospital in white coats who carry needles, give transfusions and inflict pa—" Her voice broke.

Nick's heart jolted in his chest. He pulled her to him, searing them together as she laced her arms around his neck. If there was a heaven on earth, he'd just found it. If there was a hell on earth, he'd just found that, too. But desire anchored him, sucking him down into the torrent of conflicting emotions raging inside of him.

She trusted him to find her a truth he couldn't possibly give her. He was duty bound by his promise to Governor Lockhart not to. But it was a truth his honor dictated he had to expose in order to save Caleb's life.

NEED ARCED THROUGH Grace's body like lightning, awakening every cell inside of her. It had been so long since she'd been held, too long since she'd been touched.

Leaning back, she gazed up at Nick, at the hot-blue spark of desire in his eyes. There was danger here. She knew it. But there was something else. Something she was more than anxious to explore; it didn't matter that she could get burned.

Pushing up onto her tiptoes she brushed her lips against his. She heard the file he had in his hand hit the floor behind her. He deepened the kiss, smoothing possessive hands across her back, pulling her harder against the broad expanse of his chest.

Grace moaned deep in her throat, and gave herself over to the rush, tasting him, feeling him, wanting him. Enjoying the tingle of pleasure rushing through her body like a tidal wave. She rode the crest until she felt the swell begin to dissipate.

Rocking back down onto her heels, she broke the impromptu lip-lock and sucked in a labored breath as she watched his eyelids slowly open.

What she'd just done was reckless. Out of the norm for her. Embarrassment flamed on her cheeks in hot little pools. "I— I'm—"

"Sorry," he finished for her. "Don't be. I'm not." He stepped around her, scooped up the dropped file off the floor and carried it to the bar. "I've got some paperwork for you to sign that might help us locate your birth mother."

Grace followed him over, still feeling the effects of desire in her body. Had he felt it, too? Her question was answered when he gave her a quick heated glance, before he opened the file and took out the papers.

"We'll ship this off to the attorney general of the state of Texas and hope he'll grant our request for a medical review so we can have the adoption records unsealed. It's a long shot, but we need to try this route first."

Grace swallowed, feeling disappointment bubble up from inside of her. "I pursued that avenue the moment I arrived back in Texas. My plea was denied."

"I'm sorry." His brows creased as he studied her. "I've examined the redacted copy, and short of the judge's signature on the dotted line, your mother's race and age at the time of your birth, there isn't much to go on. How old are you?"

"Thirty-three."

"Your birth mother was twenty-two when she had you. That would make her approximately fifty-five years old now. It's a long shot, but maybe we could take out an ad in the local newspaper, offer the information we have to anyone who might know who she is."

"That's a great idea. I have some money left from my parents' estate that I've been saving for an emergency. Maybe a small reward could be offered for information that leads to the discovery of her identity. If she still lives in the area, she may see herself in the ad and respond. I mean, I'm sure she gave me up out of necessity." Hope infiltrated the doubts racing around inside of her head, but Nick was right—they didn't have much to go on.

She reached out and brushed the back of Nick's strong hand where it rested against the paper.

"You still haven't told me how much your fee is."

Nick shook his head, then brought his other hand over to cover hers. "This one's on the house, sweetheart."

Touched by the gesture of kindness, she smiled at him. "I'll find a way to repay you. Cluck-cluck once a week. A clean refrigerator. Something."

"It'll be payment enough when Caleb is healthy."

Grace's heart squeezed in her chest. She needed to see that day, as well, maybe more than she needed the air in the room.

"I'm planning to drive you and Caleb to Cradles to Crayons in the morning, just in case Marshall is waiting there to pick up your trail again. I'll pick you up, as well, to make sure he doesn't follow."

She nodded. He released her hand from under his,

shuffled the worthless papers together and stuffed them into the file.

"If he's consistent, he'll eventually leave town," she said.

"What do you mean?" He looked at her, but she found her gaze slipping to his lips for an instant. She restrained herself, along with the memory of how much she'd enjoyed kissing him.

"I mean, he seems to show up out of nowhere. It usually takes me a week or so to realize he's there, watching from the shadows. He does malicious things, like letting the air out of my tires, and having the power company shut off my electricity. Then he vanishes, and I pack up and leave, afraid he'll try to hurt us someday."

"I'm planning a recon mission in Freedom tomorrow while you're at work. If he's still in town I'll find him, and convince him it would make a lot of sense if he left."

"Be careful, Nick. I'd never forgive myself if anything happened to you." Worry fisted in her stomach. "He's a cop. He's armed."

"Turn in. I'll lock up." A slow, sexy smile pulled on his mouth as he reached up to brush his fingers against the side of her face.

Grace swallowed and closed her eyes, absorbing the touch like balm, before reality snapped her back. She opened her eyes and looked at him. "Promise me?"

"You've got it. I promise."

"Thank you." She nodded, encouraged that they'd made progress on several fronts tonight, including confirmation of a physical attraction that made her feel warm clear down to her toes. But she couldn't shake her very real concerns for Nick's safety.

NICK ROCKED BACK IN HIS CHAIR and stared at his computer screen. If he sank much lower on the investigative scale he'd get dirt on his belt buckle.

Angry with himself, he considered the implications of digging deeper into Grace's past. She'd made Rodney Marshall sound like a harmless individual, whose only crimes were malicious pranks before vanishing to stalk another day. But he'd seen the damage Marshall had done in Grace's condo. He'd seen the hatred in defiling her bed with battery acid, and using bloodred spray paint on the garage wall to get his message across. He thought she was a murderer.

Rodney Marshall wasn't an average, vanilla stalker.

He pulled up the internet and plugged in the words *Billings Montana Newspapers* into the search engine.

The *Billings Gazette* popped up as the first listing. He clicked on the link, then clicked on the newspaper's archived files.

Staring at the search box he felt taunted. It begged for him to roll the dice, enter Grace's name and take a gamble on the outcome.

Nick gritted his teeth and typed *Grace Marshall* in the blank box. He hesitated, his finger on the enter key. There could be no secrets. It was all or nothing. He was preparing to go to the wall for her against the most powerful woman in the state of Texas. He had to know what Grace was running from.

He clicked Enter.

The headline filled the monitor screen.

Nick reeled back in his chair. Wild horses didn't kick as hard as the blow he felt enter his body and radiate into his heart as he reread it.

Popular Preschool Teacher Charged with Manslaughter in Husband's Death.

He hit the print request tab and closed his eyes. Sometimes you win, sometimes you lose. It was the tie he'd never anticipated.

Chapter Eight

Nick watched Grace and Caleb take the steps up to the main entrance of Cradles to Crayons.

Caleb paused on the landing, turned and waved to him.

He waved back from inside the Tahoe, and waited for them to get safely inside, before he put the vehicle in Reverse and backed out of the parking space.

Last night's internet search had produced the answer he was looking for, but it had also opened a gaping hole in his heart.

Grace Marshall had been charged with involuntary manslaughter in the death of her husband, Troy Marshall, Caleb's father. He didn't have the trial transcripts, or the nitty-gritty details of what had transpired the night Troy Marshall died, but he knew Grace had been acquitted on all charges. That explained how she'd been able to pass her background check for Cradles to Crayons. The record had no doubt been expunged by the presiding judge in the case. But why hadn't she disclosed any of it to him? Was it out of fear he would believe she was a murderer and drop her case, or the need for anonymity so she could get on with her life? He didn't know, but maybe it was some of both.

One thing was certain. The dead man's brother, Rodney Marshall, was stalking her to exact the justice he believed the court system had denied him.

Any way he figured it, Grace was in real danger. The only unknown in the equation was Caleb.

Nick's gut twisted.

Rodney Marshall's hatred had always been directed at Grace for the perceived injustice. What if he decided to go after Caleb to get to her? It was a scenario Nick had to consider; he was certain Grace had. Maybe that's why she always chose to run, rather than stay and face the terrifying possibility of Rodney Marshall someday devouring her tiny son in his hunger for vengeance.

A cold chill skittered through him. He had to find Marshall and neutralize him.

Now.

Or risk allowing harm to come to a woman and child he was falling for.

GRACE BLEW her playground whistle as hard as she could and headed straight for the swing where Lacey and Lyric Kemp were threatening to tear off each other's ponytails.

Tomboy versus princess. The Kemp twins' weekly smack-down had erupted, and it looked as though Princess Lyric might win the day with her fist wrapped in Lacey's hair.

Special-education teacher Charlotte Manning reached them first, also anxious to break up the fight while the twins still had their dark tresses intact.

"Girls. Girls. Stop this." Grace reached out and put her hand on Lyric's back. "Come on, Lyric. Let go of Lacey's hair. Let's work this out. Tell me what happened."

"She promised to give me the swing, and push me. Now she won't get off. It's my turn!"

"Is that true, Lacey? Did you promise to share with your sister?"

Lacey's scowl deepened. "Yeah," she said begrudgingly, her eyelids pulling down as her lower lip pushed out.

"A promise is a promise. You should always keep your word. Tell your sister you're sorry for not following through."

"Sorry, Lyric."

Grace reached out and put her hand on Lyric's forearm. "Let go of her and apologize for pulling her hair."

Determined but congenial, Lyric shook her hand free of her sister's ponytail, then plucked a couple of detached strands from between her fingers.

"Sorry, Lace."

A moment later they were hugging as Grace stepped back, satisfied when Lyric settled on the swing seat and Lacey gave her a push.

"Lindsay Kemp's got her hands full with those two," Charlotte Manning said as they turned to face one another.

"I agree, but thank goodness they're both reasonable children and willing to work it out." Grace scanned the playground for Caleb in the scattered clusters of children. Her aid, Tracy Sullivan, had called in sick with the flu, leaving her and Charlotte to supervise the preschool students, when they would normally have been inside in the classroom at this time of day.

"Do you see Caleb?" A measure of concern worked over her nerves that wouldn't be subdued until she laid eyes on her son. "He was playing with Zachary Giordano a moment ago in the sandbox."

Charlotte turned to assess the children. "Zachary's still there, but I don't see Caleb."

The first fingerings of panic inched up Grace's throat. "Excuse me, Charlotte."

She headed toward Zachary, a sweet little boy with Asperger's syndrome, one of many disorders in the spectrum of autism. She scanned the area for a glimpse of Caleb's green, hooded sweatshirt on the playground around her.

"Zachary?"

He stared up at her from his knees-buckled-under position on the sand, where he'd galloped his toy horse figure in a perfect circle around himself so many times, he'd dug a narrow trench in the stuff.

Her gaze fell on the discarded brown horse in the corner of the sandbox to Zachary's right.

Caleb's horse.

"Where's Caleb? Did you see where he went?" She went to her knees. "Zachary, have you seen Caleb?"

Charlotte Manning's shadow fell across the sand. "Let me, Grace. He's tactile." She closed the gap between herself and her pupil, and put her hand on Zachary's shoulder. "Zachary, I need you to point out the last place you saw Caleb go."

Like magic, Zachary seemed to come alive and a broad smile spread on his face. He raised his arm and pointed at the rear entrance into Cradles to Crayons.

"He's probably in the restroom, Grace. Go ahead, check. I can handle this alone."

"Thanks, Charlotte." Grace pushed up from her knees and hurried for the back door of the preschool. All the

safety measures and tornado-warning drills they'd practiced repeatedly, and Caleb had violated the one rule
at the top of the list. Always let a teacher know where
you're going, and take a buddy with you if possible.

She would have to reassess her methods to see if
they were truly being absorbed and understood by her
preschool students.

Someday their lives may depend on it.

Grace turned the knob and stepped into the facility's
wide rear corridor, lined with coat hooks and cubbies
for each student's personal belongings. She shut the
door and hurried for the other end where the boys' and
girls' restrooms flanked either side of the hallway. But
even before she reached them, she knew they were both
empty. There was no sliver of light coming from under
the door and gleaming against the polished tile of the
hallway. Still, she opened each door and flicked on the
light, just to be sure Caleb wasn't inside.

A solid fist of panic slammed into her brain, a myriad
of possibilities streaking through her mind. She peered
through the glass panel in the security door leading out
into the heart of the facility, where Bailey Lockhart
was currently finishing up a tour with the parents of a
prospective student.

Was it possible he'd made it through the security
door and over to the day-care wing, or back into the
classroom without being seen?

Doubt rippled through her. Cradles to Crayons' most
recent security renovations had been designed to give
the children limited access to each designated section
of the building. No toddlers from day care could wander
around in preschool classrooms and vice versa. Even the
basement had been converted into a storm cellar.

Grace's heart rate increased as she opened the door and stepped out into the corridor that ran between the classrooms and the day care.

"Excuse me, Ms. Lockhart, may I speak with you?"

Bailey looked up and smiled. "Certainly." She handed the young couple a Cradles to Crayons brochure. "This will explain all of the early-childhood programs we offer. If you'd like to look it over for a moment, I'll be right back."

"Grace?" Bailey said in a voice just above a whisper. "Is something wrong?"

Tension twisted Grace's muscles into knots, but she smiled at her boss in spite of her desire to call out the National Guard. "Have you by any chance seen Caleb? He's missing from the playground."

"No, I haven't. I've been showing the Johnsons around the facility. Have you checked with day care?"

"That's my next stop."

"Keep me posted. I'm sure he's here somewhere."

Grace nodded and headed for the day care, certain that Caleb wouldn't have gone there. He'd jumped for joy last year when he escaped to preschool. Still, she needed to check. At the Dutch door, with the top half open, she stopped and peered in. One of the attendants, Pamela Maxwell, was reading a book to the entire group of little ones, but Caleb wasn't among them.

Turning, Grace headed back down the corridor. Just past the door with the words *Storm Cellar* on it, she pulled up short. They'd drilled dozens of times on what to do if the tornado-warning siren sounded. Take cover in the shelter and wait for the twister to pass.

Grace pulled open the door.

The automatic emergency lighting switched on.

She took the broad stairway down into the basement two steps at a time, and hurried to the concrete, steel-reinforced storm cellar, capable of withstanding a direct hit by an F5 tornado with the blast door shut.

She stepped inside and looked around the cavernous room. Stacked in one corner was a pallet of bottled water and a few food rations. A child could easily hide behind the emergency supplies.

"Caleb! Are you in here? Caleb Marshall!" No answer.

"Oh, dear God," she whispered, her body beginning to shake. Children didn't just vanish into thin air. Her throat squeezed as she raced from the room and pounded up the stairs, cursing Rodney Marshall.

He wouldn't hurt him, would he? His own flesh and blood?

She bolted through the doorway and collided with Bailey.

"Grace."

"We need to call the police. Caleb's gone!" The choked request rolled out of her mouth as she shoved her hand into her sweater pocket and locked her fingers around her cell phone.

She shouldn't have stayed in Freedom. She should have run the second Rodney found them. Her worst nightmare was playing out in raw reality right in front of her and she was helpless to stop it. She needed Nick. Now.

"Grace."

She focused on her boss for an instant, on the tone of concern in her voice, and the sympathetic smile that spread on her mouth.

"Caleb's fine. The Johnsons nearly tripped over him

when they were leaving. He's sitting out on the front steps."

"How?" Grace whispered, her hand going to her heart as it thudded against her palm and nearly pounded out of her chest.

"I showed the Johnsons the coat-and-belongings corridor, and they wanted to look out over the playground. I made the mistake of leaving the security door ajar. He must have been in the bathroom at the time and simply slipped out into the hallway. From there it was simple to cross to the main entrance and go outside."

"Thank God he's okay." Grace swallowed hard. "I'll go…and talk to him. He certainly knows better than to leave the building without permission."

Bailey squeezed her hand. "I'm so sorry, Grace. I'll find a way to make sure something like this never happens again."

"I know you will." She smiled at the boss who'd become her friend, and turned for the tile-lined corridor leading to the front entrance. Pausing next to the doorjamb, she stared out the window in the door, at where Caleb sat on the landing, gazing at the parking lot.

Grace sucked in a deep breath and let go of her fear. He was safe, that's all that mattered, but she still intended to scold him for not following the safety rules, and encourage him to do better next time. Turning the knob, she pushed the door open and went outside.

"There you are," she said. "Mommy was worried when I couldn't find you on the playground." She closed the door and took a spot next to him, wrapping her arms around her knees. "What are you doing out here?"

"Waiting."

"For what?"

"It's who," Caleb insisted, shielding his eyes from the sun as he smiled up at her. "Mister Nick is coming to get us. I don't wanna miss him."

Grace's heart sagged in her chest. Hot tears stung the back of her eyes, but she blinked them away, wondering if she was doing the right thing, staying in Freedom, allowing Nick and Caleb's attachment to solidify.

"Oh, sweetheart, come here. We won't miss Nick. He'll be here, and I bet he'll even come inside if he can't find us." Reaching over at a sideways angle, she pulled him onto her lap, and started when a small red-and-yellow toy snake jiggled halfway out of his sweatshirt pocket.

She'd never seen the creepy toy before and it didn't look like anything he'd picked up at Cradles to Crayons.

"Where'd you get that ugly thing? Did Zachary-G give it to you?"

Caleb reached down, pulled the toy out of his pocket by its head and wiggled it back and forth, watching its rubbery body ripple.

"What's a Uncle Rodney?"

Blood iced in her veins.

"Inside, Caleb. Let's go inside." Grace hauled her son up from the steps with her, locking her arms around him as she glanced around, looking for Rodney Marshall's white Chevy.

"Wait! I want Mister Nick," Caleb protested, as she backed them toward the door, grasped the knob, pulled it open and hurried inside.

NICK CLOSED HIS CELL PHONE, shot a glance in his side mirror and pulled back out onto the street.

His early-morning grid search of Freedom hadn't yielded a single sign of Rodney Marshall's white Chevy. Now he knew why.

A blade of anxiety knifed through him. Marshall had been right under his nose and he'd missed the scent. Worse yet he'd gotten close to Caleb. The message he'd sent to Grace along with the toy snake was inherently clear.

Rodney Marshall could get to her son anytime he wanted to.

Not if Nick had anything to do with it.

Nick stepped down on the accelerator, hurried across town and ten minutes later pulled into the parking lot of Cradles to Crayons, where parents were in the process of picking up their children.

Nosing the Tahoe into a parking space, he climbed out and immediately spotted Grace standing at the base of the steps, supervising the orderly exit of her pupils into their parents' waiting arms.

His heart jolted in his chest when she caught sight of him and they made eye contact. Like an addict desperate for his next fix, he focused on her, and her alone.

"Hey, Nick. How are you?" Lindsay Kemp stood in his path.

"Never better." He paused to glance down at her and Wade's cute twin daughters, who were having a hard time standing still despite their mom's tight grip on their hands. They looked up at him with snapping brown eyes, and he couldn't help but notice their messy ponytails. They were clearly a handful of willpower, he decided as he grinned at them. "Hi, girls."

"Are you Mister Nick?"

"Yeah." Caleb must have relayed the information to

them, probably as part of a horse tale. Flattered, he re-established eye contact with Lindsay.

"I'm putting together the Community Thanksgiving Luncheon and I know your family lives in Idaho. You'll probably be staying in Freedom like the rest of the CSaI agents because of recent troubles for the governor. But will you come and join us? No one should be alone during the holiday."

Like a magnet, Nick's gaze wandered back to Grace as she released the last child to his parent.

He didn't plan on being alone this year.

"What's the date?"

"November 23, at the community center. Noon."

"Sure. I'll try to make it. Thanks for the invite." Nodding to her, he resumed his march across the parking lot, bent on reaching Grace.

He was desperate to satisfy the physical desire burning inside of him, as much as his emotional need to comfort her. To reassure her that he could, and would, protect her and Caleb from Rodney Marshall even if it meant he never let them out of his sight again.

Mesmerized, he closed the distance, watching loose strands of her blond hair tangle in the Texas wind. Her blue-eyed gaze locked on his with an unwavering intensity that sent a charge through him.

Grace Marshall was a beautiful woman. He was helpless to suppress the rush of desire that slammed into his body with the force of a hurricane.

"Grace. Are you okay?"

She smiled up at him, but fear widened her eyes when she diverted her gaze to scan the parking lot behind him before she refocused her attention on him. "I am now that you're here. Come inside. I've made a decision."

Nick followed Grace up the steps and into the building. "Where's Caleb?"

"He's safe in day care until I'm finished here."

"Finished?"

She stopped in the corridor.

Grace's heart threatened to pound out of her chest. Reaching out, she put her hand on his forearm. "Let's go to my classroom. It's quiet there. I have something to tell you."

The feel of Nick's hand pressed against her back provided a measure of comfort as she pointed to the first classroom on the right and stepped inside, closing the door behind him.

He looked around the room and immediately walked over to her desk, where he thumped the box she'd packed her things up in, before turning to study her.

"What's going on? You're running again?" The glint in his eyes hardened, a wall of steel-blue she'd have to forge.

"I always knew the day would come when Rodney would figure out that threatening Caleb was the only way he could truly torment me. And I've always lived up to his expectations like a timid animal, rather than fight, but I can't run this time. Caleb will die if I don't stay in Freedom to find my birth mother."

Nick's expression softened as he stepped toward her. Reaching out, he brushed his fingers against her cheek, sending a wisp of heat across her skin. "So why the box?"

"I've asked Bailey for a temporary leave of absence. She has agreed. She believes it's solely because of Caleb's worsening condition, and it is to some extent, but I know we're not safe here anymore. It's one less point of contact for Rodney."

"You know I'm not going to let either one of you out of my sight again. Trust me, Grace, when I tell you I'll find a way to stop Marshall."

Hope worked through her thoughts as she gazed up at Nick's handsome face and saw the determined set of his jaw. He made her feel safe, but she hadn't told him everything. Hadn't been as honest as she needed to be if she expected him to stand by her, and damn the consequences if anyone in Freedom ever found out her dark secret.

She cared for Nick Cavanaugh. Caleb did, too. Nick was all he'd talked about for days. She hadn't planned to feel like this, but she did. And now there was no going back to the way things were before he'd come roaring into their lives.

Grace's throat closed on the confession she needed to exorcise. Swallowing her hesitation, she leaned back on her desk for support and forced the words out into the open between them.

"I've kept something from you. Something horrific from my past, but only because I couldn't risk letting it destroy the very real chance you'll find my birth mother before it's too late."

"Grace, I—"

"Please let me finish," she whispered, raising her hand, stopping him from touching her when he reached out. She couldn't let him touch her, not yet. Not without knowing what his response would be once he found out what a horrible thing she'd done. What a murderous thing….

She saw Nick's mouth close on his words through a screen of hot tears she was powerless to stop.

"Rodney Marshall wants revenge because I killed his brother…. I killed my husband, Troy."

Chapter Nine

"In self-defense, Grace." Nick gathered her against his chest in a single heartbeat. She was pliant and willing, until his verbal confession sank into her mind and produced the push-back he knew would come. It was a price he was eager to pay in order to gain back a measure of his honor.

"You knew?" She put an arm's length between them. "And you didn't question me?"

"You're being threatened, Grace. By a man who's sworn to uphold the law, not skirt it. The word *murderer* spray painted on the back of your garage wall and battery acid spewed all over your bedroom convinced me there was more going on than you were willing, or able to tell me." He sucked in a deep breath to release the tension building inside his body.

"I'd be negligent in doing my job if I hadn't looked into your background. I care about you and Caleb. I was willing to wait for an explanation, but only for so long."

He wasn't sure where she weighed in on the emotional scale at the moment, but her chin came up in defiance as she stared at him through teary blue eyes. He watched her lower lip quiver for an instant. The tell. The opening crack in her tough facade?

"Does this mean you're willing to retain my case? Because you're free to decline if you'd like."

"I'm not the declining kind, sweetheart."

In a couple of steps she was in his arms again. Right where he needed her to be.

HE WAS TOO DAMNED EXCITED to eat, but he pulled open Nick Cavanaugh's refrigerator as if he owned it and stared inside. A gallon of milk, a couple of yogurts—who ate that crap anyway? Eggs…too much work. Besides they came in a dozen—easy for Cavanaugh to notice if a couple went missing…. Kitchen smells were a dead giveaway. Veggies in the crisper, too much work….

His perusal fell on a clear plastic container sitting on the bottom shelf. Reaching in, he grabbed it, letting the door swing shut as he stepped back and lifted the lid just enough to take a whiff.

"Mmm." It sure smelled as if the mystery woman, who'd moved her suitcase into one of the spare bedrooms along with her brat, knew how to cook, because Cavanaugh sure as hell didn't.

Fingering a piece of the meat, he picked it up and took a bite, savoring the exotic flavors of cayenne pepper, fenugreek and turmeric melded in the curry-blend coating. Hell, yeah, he'd cooked stuff like this before, back in Iraq, back before things went to hell in a handbasket.

Six bites and it was gone. He picked up the other piece and downed it, too, feeling gut-bomb full as he wiped his hand across his mouth and checked the floor for crumbs.

With three of them in the house now, the sink was a safe bet to ditch the evidence that he'd ever been there. Not that it was going to matter after today. He was clearing out. His IEDs were built, packed and ready to go; there wasn't any reason to hang around and risk detection, just so he could steal food, shower and play with explosives in a CSaI agent's house.

Stepping across the kitchen in his stocking feet, he put the container in the empty sink, turned on the water, rinsed his hands and dried them off on the dish towel folded neatly on the counter.

Then just for fun, he wadded it up and left it where he'd found it.

It was almost go-time, but he damn sure needed a shower.

"I DON'T KNOW HOW he got past me." Nick glanced over at Grace sitting in the passenger seat. Caleb was in the back strapped in his car seat, trotting a plastic horse over every surface around him.

"I worked a grid search this morning, never saw his car."

"That's his, what do you call it? M.O. Harass, elude, then disappear."

"If the Chevy is still in this county, Sheriff Hale's local APB will find it. He's got his deputies on the lookout."

"Did you tell him about my past?"

"Only need-to-know information. Hale was sympathetic, said Rodney's Montana badge don't mean nothin' in Texas."

She let out an audible sigh. "I pray you're right, Nick. I hope he really is gone. I think he uses vacation time from his department in Billings. He takes a week or two and makes my life hell, then heads home to write traffic tickets and crime reports until the next time he can intrude into our lives."

He reached over and touched her arm. "Relax. Everyone's on their toes now. He doesn't have anonymity anymore. When you shine the light on snakes, they usually slither into their holes."

Grace glanced over at Nick, enjoying the feel of his reassuring hand on her forearm. She just wished she could be as certain as he was. That her sense of an inevitable face-to-face confrontation with her ex-brother-in-law sometime in the future would melt away into oblivion, but she'd been preparing for it for a long time.

"Thank you for supper." Nick had taken them out to the Talk of the Town Café for dinner.

"You're welcome. Valerio grills a mean steak."

"I'm looking forward to working with him and Faith. There's a great group of people at Talk of the Town."

"When do you start?"

"Monday at 6:00 p.m."

"You know I'll cover Caleb on the evenings you work."

"You don't look like the babysitter type."

"Yeah, well, I'm the oldest of four brothers. I'm equipped to show him the ropes." Nick slowed the vehicle and eased up next to a mailbox at the head of the driveway leading into the ranch.

He took his hand off of her arm, put the Tahoe in Park and hit the auto-down button for the window.

She instantly missed the feel of his fingers on her skin and battled back a surge of desire hot enough that it burned embarrassment into her cheeks.

"If it's scrapping, or tactical training on how to pick up his dirty socks without touching them, I can handle

Play the Lucky 7 Hearts Game

and get...
2 FREE BOOKS and
2 FREE MYSTERY GIFTS...
YOURS TO KEEP!

yes! I have scratched off the gold card.
Please send me my **2 FREE BOOKS** and
2 FREE MYSTERY GIFTS (gifts are worth about $10).
I understand that I am under no obligation to purchase
any books as explained on the back of this card.

Scratch Here!
Then look below to see what your
cards get you...*2 Free Books*
& 2 Free Mystery Gifts!

☐ I prefer the regular-print edition
182/382 HDL FJCE

☐ I prefer the larger-print edition
199/399 HDL FJCE

FIRST NAME   LAST NAME

ADDRESS

APT.#   CITY

STATE/PROV.   ZIP/POSTAL CODE

Visit us online at
www.ReaderService.com

Twenty-one gets you
2 FREE BOOKS and
2 FREE MYSTERY GIFTS!

Twenty gets you
2 FREE BOOKS!

Nineteen gets you
1 FREE BOOK!

TRY AGAIN!

Offer limited to one per household and not applicable to series that subscriber is currently receiving.

Your Privacy—The Reader Service is committed to protecting your privacy. Our Privacy Policy is available online at www.ReaderService.com or upon request from the Reader Service. We make a portion of our mailing list available to reputable third parties that offer products we believe may interest you. If you prefer that we not exchange your name with third parties, or if you wish to clarify or modify your communication preferences, please visit us at www.ReaderService.com/consumerschoice or write to us at Reader Service Preference Service, P.O. Box 9062, Buffalo, NY 14269. Include your complete name and address.

▼ **DETACH AND MAIL CARD TODAY!** ▼

H-I-11/11

it." He opened the box and took out the mail, then tossed it on the dash in front of him, before closing the box and turning to look at Caleb in the backseat.

"What do you say, buddy? You and me, holding down the fort while your mom works at the café?"

"I say yeah!" Caleb grinned, held up his toy horse and galloped it in the air. "Can we ride like this?"

"Sure can."

"Neee-heee." Caleb attempted to duplicate the sound of a whinny, then repeated the high-pitched call. "Neee-heee."

She laughed at the odd little noise, turning in amusement to look at her son. "What just came out of that horse's mouth?" She widened her eyes and let her mouth gape open in surprise.

Caleb grinned, proud of his skills. "Zachary-G told me that's the sound horses make."

"Good job. We'll hang out at the corral on Saturday and you can perfect it. I'll bet old Jericho will talk back to you. What do you say?"

"Okay." Caleb let his head lull back against the headrest, still grinning at Nick, but she could see his energy level beginning to wane, and hoped he'd be able to hold out until the weekend so he could enjoy talking to Nick's horses.

Nick turned back around, rolled up the window, put the rig in gear and pulled into the drive.

Settling back in her seat, she let an odd sensation of comfort build inside her heart and spread to her entire body. She couldn't remember the last time she'd felt this secure; she had the man in the driver's seat next to her to thank for it. He was all about strength, honor and sex appeal. If she didn't know anything else about him, she knew that.

NICK TRAINED HIS FOCUS on the darkening drive in front of him, on the discernible shadows of dusk gathering at the edges of the gravel lane. He reached down and flipped on his headlights, catching a brief flit of movement in his left peripheral vision.

Unease flooded his system, raising his caution level a notch.

Stepping on the brake pedal, he brought the SUV to a stop.

"What is it?" Grace asked, glancing over at him.

"I'm not sure." He put the rig in Reverse, stared into the side mirror and backed up twenty feet to an opening in the curtain of Texas sage they'd just passed.

"But I swear I saw someone run between a couple of sage." Staring at the exact spot he believed he'd seen someone or something, he tried to pick them out amongst the patches of upland switchgrass and prickly pear dotting the rolling landscape.

Movement sucked his attention to a scrub oak where a whitetail buck raked his antlers against its trunk with violent strokes.

"Look, Grace." He pointed. "He's trying to shed his horns after breeding season. I'll have to bring Caleb out here to see if we can locate them before the coyotes drag them off to chew on."

"He'd like that, wouldn't you, Caleb?" She turned slightly to look into the backseat. "He's sound asleep, Nick. I suppose it will have to wait until tomorrow."

"It's been a rough day for the little guy." Nick put the Tahoe in Drive and took his foot off the brake pedal.

The deer's movements were probably what he'd seen. Its sandy-brown hide matched the glint of color on the edge of his headlight beams, but as he eased down on the gas pedal, he realized he couldn't be certain. For half a second, he thought he'd seen a man standing upright, wearing desert camouflage. The same broken tawny pattern he'd learned to identify with precise accuracy in Iraq. A skill he'd used a hundred times in his recon missions to avoid walking into an ambush.

Unease raked over his nerves, bringing his senses to a heightened state of alert he couldn't ignore. What would a man in camo be doing on the ranch besides trespassing? Was it possible Rodney Marshall had discovered Grace's location and was waiting to confirm her identity when she climbed out of his vehicle? Still, based on his proximity to the ranch house it appeared the man had been running in the opposite direction.

Nick's guard was up when he pulled into the circle drive in front of the house and killed the engine. He didn't plan on letting it down until they were safely inside.

He snagged the mail off the dash, climbed out and went around to the passenger side, where Grace unbuckled Caleb and took him out of his car seat.

"Here. Let me." Nick pulled the little boy into his arms and handed Grace the mail along with his keys. "After you." He glanced around the perimeter for visible threats, and fell in behind her up the walk to the front door. "It's the brass one in the middle."

He watched Grace push the designated key into the lock and turn it, but he never heard the click of the locks release.

"That's strange," Grace said as she removed the key and turned to stare up at him. "The door was already unlocked. I know I saw you lock it this morning when we left for Cradles to Crayons."

"Back to the car," Nick ordered, feeling his muscles tense in anticipation of a fight. "I want you and Caleb safe. I'm going to clear the house, make sure there's no one inside."

He followed her off the step landing, down the walkway and back to the vehicle with Caleb clutched in his arms. Was it possible Rodney Marshall had found a way in? It had the markings of his M.O.—get in, wreak havoc, get out. But where did the elusive man in camo fit in?

"Passenger-side rear door."

Grace pulled it open and slipped into the seat.

Nick eased Caleb onto his mother's lap. "I'll get my weapon out of the glove box. Use the fob on the key ring to lock the doors from the inside. If anyone comes close, press the panic button, and I'll come running."

"Okay." Grace nodded, brushing her hand across Caleb's head as she stared down at him.

"Grace." Nick reached out and touched her face, then eased her chin up with his fingertips so he could look into her eyes. "It's going to be okay."

A trail of tears on her cheeks glistened in the overhead light.

"I promise I'll never let anything happen to you, or to Caleb. No one's going to hurt you again." Nick released her, stepped back and shut the door.

Moving quickly, he opened the passenger-side front door, then the glove box, and took out his holstered weapon. He clipped it on his belt, stepped back and closed the door, hearing the auto-locks clamp down.

Safe.

Turning, he slipped into the growing darkness and approached the front door with his senses on full alert.

Maybe they'd been too confident that Marshall had skipped town. So why hadn't Sheriff Hale's APB produced his white Chevy? Unless he'd already changed vehicles.

Nick took the steps, paused on the landing next to the front door and unholstered his weapon. Reaching out, he turned the knob and eased the front door open just enough to slip inside.

Light spilled out of the hallway into the foyer, giving him ample visibility. He closed the door without a sound and pressed the security code into the alarm pad. If Rodney Marshall was still inside the house, he wasn't getting out in silence. He planned to nail him to the wall until Sheriff Hale took him away in a pair of handcuffs. Marshall would never threaten Grace or Caleb again as long as he was sucking air.

Nick turned to his right and cleared the kitchen and dining room, noting the range-hood light was on over the stove. He didn't recall leaving it on this morning when he'd made Grace and Caleb a pancake.

The hair on the back of his neck bristled as he turned around and headed along the hallway.

Sucking up next to the wall, he leaned out and cleared the living room over his pistol sights, moved past and headed for the bedroom section of the sprawling ranch-style house, most of which he rarely ever ventured into. One by one he flipped on the light switches and cleared each bedroom, including the one he used as an office. Grace and Caleb's room hadn't been disturbed. If Marshall had broken into the house, their room should have been the one he homed in on.

Hesitating outside the closed door to the fifth bedroom, he couldn't recall the last time he'd even opened the door on it, but maybe Rodney Marshall had.

Nick turned the knob, pushed the door open, stepped inside and flicked on the light, scanning the large bedroom over his pistol sight.

A wave of apprehension glanced over him as he pulled in a long breath to dissect the lingering smells in the room.

Fresh air tinged with Texas sage.

Musky deodorant.

Shampoo.

In five strides he reached the window and jerked the cord on the blinds.

The bottom of the window pane was open several inches, allowing a rush of air to come in. A window that was wired into the security system and should have set off the alarm. The sensor wire had no doubt been cut. He pushed up on the window and spotted the tiny alligator clip someone had used to bypass the alarm.

Nick turned for the adjacent bathroom, switched on the light and stared at the interior. A blade of realization carved through his body.

Beads of water clung to the shower walls and a band of steam on the bottom of the vanity mirror hadn't evaporated yet.

"What the hell?" He moved inside and felt the towel hanging on the towel bar.

It was still damp.

They'd just missed stepping on whoever had been inside his house by less than fifteen minutes.

The man in camouflage he'd seen along the driveway into the ranch?

Backtracking, Nick closed and latched the window,

then killed the lights and left the room, anxious to get Grace and Caleb safely inside, in spite of his unwelcome houseguest's lingering presence. He'd put a wedge in the window so the intruder couldn't use it for access if they came back. Setting the alarm from now on would be standard operating procedure, and he'd let Sheriff Hale know an odd intruder had broken into his house to take a shower. But in spite of the creepiness factor associated with it, he couldn't dispel the worry knotting in his gut.

This had nothing to do with Grace or Caleb Marshall, and everything to do with his position at Corps Security and Investigations. Whoever had sudsed up in one of his showers half an hour ago knew his daily routine.

GRACE HELD CALEB a little tighter and stared into the night, waiting for any sign of Nick emerging from the house. Relaxing was out of the question; in fact, she'd been figuratively holding her breath from the moment he'd exited the vehicle, and she'd possibly destroyed the key fob in her hand with perspiration and pressure.

Twin globe-encased lights on either side of the front door came on, flooding the steps and walkway with illumination.

Her heartbeat slowed as she watched him step outside into the light and walk toward the Tahoe in even strides. He was a good man. An honorable man. A man she wanted in her and Caleb's lives.

Hand trembling, she fingered the alarm button and disengaged the door locks for him.

He lifted the handle and pulled open the Tahoe's door. "All clear. Let's get inside. I'll take Caleb." Nick gently lifted him from her arms and stepped back so she could climb out and shut the door.

"Do you think Rodney found our location?"

"No." His answer was straightforward, but she wasn't sure how he could be so decisive.

Taking the lead with the fob in one hand and Nick's mail in her other, she headed for the house, anxious to get inside.

They stepped into the foyer and she closed the door behind them.

"Do you remember how to set the alarm?" he asked, turning toward her.

"Yes."

"Set it now, and every time you're here."

A measure of concern filled up her insides as she looked up at him. "Something's wrong, isn't it?"

He nodded. "Someone has been in the house. They gained access through a window in the last bedroom on the right. I don't want to take any chances if they come back and try to get in at another point of entry. The alarm will set off a warning and get Sheriff Hale out here."

"What makes you think it isn't Rodney again?"

"Your room is intact." He turned and headed down the hallway, leaving her to set the security alarm. A moment later he returned.

She handed him the mail and his key ring. Their fingers brushed in the exchange and before she could move, he pulled her against his chest.

Grace closed her eyes, letting the pleasurable sensation of touching him smooth the fear from her nerves. He had a risky job. There were times when he was in physical danger. Times when his life could be threatened. Unnerved, she pushed back, anxious to secure details about his job at CSaI, but before she could get a single question out, his lips were on hers.

Nick tasted good…and hungry, just like she was. Arching against him, she set off a moan deep in the back of his throat.

He parted her lips with his tongue and explored her mouth in desire-provoking sweeps, until she thought she'd come apart in his arms.

Grace breathed him in, clinging to every sensation he aroused in her willing body. She'd been alone too long. She'd suffered the betrayal of abuse by her dead husband. She'd traveled too many miles without someone in her life, and in that instant of reflection, she mentally crossed the line. It was time to trust again. To trust Nick Cavanaugh with her safety, and her body.

Nick felt it. Felt the moment she surrendered herself to him. Dazed, he ended the kiss to gaze down into her face. Her eyes gleamed with anticipation.

"You're beautiful, Grace," he whispered, watching a seductive smile bow her sexy, swollen lips reddened from contact with his. He wanted more.

"You're not so bad yourself, Nick Cavanaugh," she whispered back. "I'm going to put Caleb in his pajamas and tuck him in." She turned and left him standing in the foyer.

He watched her until she slipped into the bedroom, then turned and headed for the kitchen, where he tossed the mail on the bar and looked around before heading to the cupboard for a glass. He pulled one out, turned to the sink and raised the faucet handle. Water streamed into a container he knew he hadn't emptied. The one he'd put Grace's leftover curry chicken into the night before.

Not only had the intruder used the shower, he'd been stealing food. What else had he done here?

Agitated, Nick filled his glass to the brim and guzzled the water. He planned to keep his weapon an arm's length away, until he figured out who'd invaded his home.

Finished, he set the glass in the sink next to the container and walked to the bar where he picked up the envelope on top, glanced at the Holy Cross Hospital return address and tore it open.

Dear Mr. Cavanaugh,
We regret to inform you that you are not a bone-marrow match for Caleb Marshall. Thank you for submitting yourself to the testing procedure.
Sincerely,
Melissa Johnson
Donor Registry Coordinator

"He's out like a light," Grace announced from behind him.

Nick turned at the sound of her voice and casually slid the letter onto the counter behind him. He'd known at the time he took the test that his blood type was standard fare, but it still gave him a pang of regret deep in his chest knowing he couldn't help Caleb himself.

"I'm planning to take you both riding on Saturday. Do you think he can hold out until then?"

She moved in close to him. "Yes, if we take it easy."

He reached for her and pulled her into his arms, where he breathed in the light, honey-sweet smell of her hair; he was just about to kiss her when she pulled back and snagged the letter off of the bar.

"Oh, Nick. I had no idea you'd done this." She smiled up at him. "Thank you."

"You're welcome. Unfortunately, I'm not a match."

"Not many people are."

He reached for her again, but she took his hand instead and tugged him along with her into the hallway. At his bedroom door, she paused to gaze up at him. "I don't want to be alone tonight, Nick."

"Are you sure?"

"Yes." She turned the knob, pushed the door open and pulled him inside.

Hungry to touch her, he swept her up into his arms and carried her to the bed, where he put her down on the comforter. Then he stripped off his shirt.

Mesmerized, he watched her work the buttons on her blouse, pull it off, reach down and unhook the front closure on her bra. His mouth went dry as she peeled back the shimmery fabric to expose her perfectly rounded breasts, peaked with taut nipples he wanted to taste.

Heat set fire to his body as he shed his jeans, then slowly lay down with her. He stroked his fingertips along her arm and devoured her mouth hungrily.

Deep sighs rose in her throat as she brushed her hands across his back and arched beneath him.

He pulled back for an instant of sanity. "You're sure this is what you want, Grace?"

She turned sleepy eyes on him and smiled. "I don't want to be alone tonight, and you don't, either. Let's enjoy each other. Please."

Reaching down, he undid the buttons and slid the zipper on her jeans, then, slipping his hand inside, he pushed them down over her bottom.

"You're so incredible," he whispered, visually consuming every luscious curve of her body before he rolled her underneath him.

He suddenly didn't care if morning never came.

Chapter Ten

Nick settled himself at the table and took a swig of coffee from his travel mug. Coffee Grace had made for them this morning after their night of whispers and pleasure in the dark.

Desire invaded his thoughts as he mentally recalled every detail of her silky body.

He reached down and flipped open the file in front of him, anxious for a distraction. He'd be no good this morning if he didn't find a way to put the memory to rest for the time being.

Looking up, he watched each CSaI team member file into the conference room and take their seats around the table for Nolan's discovery briefing.

Nolan was the last one in, closing the door behind him. He looked exhausted. His skin was tinged a shade of gray that Nick hadn't seen before. Odd, he thought, considering that D.C. was Nolan's hometown. He should have been energized by the visit.

"Good morning, gentlemen. I trust you've each collected the intel we need to keep Governor Lockhart safe."

The members each flipped through their file folders.

"Wade, what do we have on Wes Bradley?" Nolan asked as he pulled out his chair and sat down.

"Wesley James Bradley entered the U.S. Marine Corps in December 2006. He was reported killed in an IED attack six months ago in Iraq," Wade said, staring at the paperwork in front of him before looking up.

Nolan leaned forward and put his elbows on the table. "Did you get anything on the cell-tower records from Sheriff Hale?"

"Yes. The tower transmissions put Wes Bradley in Freedom the day of the shooting, but the cell phone he used was a throwaway. It was turned off the next day. I also found out that Lewis and Bradley were in Iraq at the same time." Wade rocked back in his chair. "They might have known each other, and if they did, Lewis would have known that Bradley was dead."

"Which would make Wes Bradley a perfect alias for whoever took those shots at Governor Lockhart," Nick said, ready to jump into the session with both feet now that he'd contained his thoughts in regards to Grace.

Matteo rapped his knuckles on the table a couple of times. "Trevor Lewis was a member of the group that bombed the governor's announcement of her presidential run. Do you suppose whoever is using Wes Bradley's name as an alias is also a member?"

"Could be. But they're an underground organization. Pretty tough to nail down any kind of membership roster, much less know how many cells there could be out there," Nick surmised.

"Let's pull a list of all the men in Bradley's unit. Do a soft track on where they are now. Maybe we'll get lucky and be able to find one individual they all have in common," Nolan said. "And, Wade, get in touch with the Marine Corps department for death notification. I want to know how Wes Bradley's remains were handled. There's a chance he could still be alive."

"I'll get right on it."

"Parker, anything more on the shooter at Twin Harts Ranch?" Nolan asked.

"We're pretty sure we caught a frame of him on surveillance working the perimeter outside the house. Nick and Matteo confirmed that his build matches that of the man they saw at Holy Cross the day Lewis died."

"Is that so?" Nolan asked, his brows pulling together as he contemplated the implications. "Did he leave any evidence behind?"

"A boot print," Matteo said. "We made a casting of it. Standard-issue Marine Corps."

Nolan's eyes narrowed. "We could be dealing with one of our own."

"Looks that way." Matt sat back in his chair as a hush settled over the room.

Nick cursed under his breath. No one wanted to believe a brother in arms had turned, but it was starting to seem as though that could be the case.

"Good work, everybody, on the Bradley angle." Nolan pulled a stack of paper from his file, took the top one and passed the rest to his right. "But we've got another assignment. Governor Lockhart has decided to hold a press conference a week before Thanksgiving to announce a new early-childhood reading program, centered on community involvement. The location she has chosen gives me heartburn, but she insists it's the best place. The announcement goes out in tomorrow's papers."

Nick took his copy and read the brief paragraph of information, feeling a knot take up space in his gut. "Cradles to Crayons?"

"Yes. I tried to convince her to announce it in Freedom's town square, but she didn't like the logistical look. She believes a preschool classroom is the ideal setting. It's scheduled for Thursday at two in the afternoon. She'll take the front of the class, give a brief speech on the dynamics of the program, then open it up for questions from the press. Seating will be limited to fifty people inside, and a hundred and fifty outside in the parking lot. Classes and day care will dismiss early, with only one class of four-year-olds and their teacher in attendance at the actual speech. I want each and every one of you there with your eyes open and your game on. I don't anticipate trouble, but we need to be prepared for anything."

Nick relaxed slightly. With Grace taking a leave of absence from the preschool, she wouldn't be required to be there, and if she stayed home, Caleb would, too.

"The entire team will do a sweep two hours before the event. Sheriff Hale and his deputies will monitor the entrance and exit into the parking lot, as well as directing traffic."

"My twins attend. Maybe I'll ask Lindsay to keep them home," Wade said.

"Let's just make sure we conduct a thorough threat assessment." Nolan shuffled his paperwork together and closed the file. "Any questions?"

"How was D.C.?" Nick glanced at his friend, waiting to see if Nolan's true feelings about the trip would show on his face. They came out when his eyes narrowed in contemplation and his mouth drooped.

"It's cold this time of year. Other than that, it's business as usual. Politicians spending our money like it belongs to them."

Nick nodded in agreement. "Glad to have you home, sir."

Nolan's gaze locked with Nick's and a measure of understanding passed between them.

Something was wrong.

Nolan's former life had been in D.C., and Nick wasn't sure exactly what kind of ghosts still resided there, but something was haunting Nolan Law.

"Thank you, Cavanaugh. Gentlemen, you're dismissed." Nolan scooped up the file and left the room.

Nick wasn't far behind him, suddenly anxious to see Grace and Caleb. Thank goodness he didn't have long to wait: as he stepped out of the conference room and walked to the seating area in front of Amelia's desk, he saw them waiting for him. He paused for a moment, watching as Grace read a storybook to her son, who sat on her lap leaning his head against her shoulder.

His heart twisted in his chest. He had to do something to save Caleb. Walk through fire, chew glass, speak to Governor Lockhart again?

Grace glanced up, her blue-eyed gaze focused on him alone. She smiled; he smiled back and moved toward them.

"Finished?" she asked, closing the book.

"Yeah."

Caleb climbed down off his mother's lap and without hesitation bolted forward with a broad grin on his face.

"Mister Nick!" he yelled, hopping at the last possible second for Nick to snag him and swing him up into his arms.

"Hey, buddy, ya ready to go?"

"Yeah."

"How about we go on a picnic this afternoon? Get some fresh air and sunshine?"

Caleb nodded. "Eat Goldfish?"

"Goldfish?"

"It's a cracker, Nick. Shaped like a fish," Grace clarified, smiling up at them both.

"I love them," Caleb said as he let his cheek rest against Nick's shoulder.

He was beginning to love something, too, but it wasn't Goldfish.

NICK TIGHTENED THE CINCH on Jericho, then checked the leather bags he'd secured to the back of the saddle. The satchels were loaded with a picnic lunch consisting of PB and J sandwiches Caleb had proudly helped his mother slap together, apple juice boxes and a bag of Goldfish crackers, all delectable foods to a four-year-old, or so he'd been told in the grocery-store aisle.

He'd eat dirt if it meant getting to enjoy the afternoon with Grace and Caleb.

Skirting the back of his horse, he helped her pull the cinch tight on Tulip, a gentle quarter-horse mare in a beautiful shade of chestnut. "She won't give you any trouble. She's kid gentle." He gazed down at her as he lowered the stirrup from off the saddle horn. "Do you know how to ride?"

"I was born in Texas, wasn't I?"

He grinned. "Well, take it easy on me, then, will ya?"

"Never." Her smile faded slowly as she stared up at him, and he resisted the overwhelming urge to kiss her on the spot, to feel her willing body respond to his on a level he'd never experienced before last night.

Glancing away, he looked at Caleb where he stood next to the corral, leaning on the second rung, wearing the pair of new cowboy boots they'd picked up after their trip to the grocery store. "He looks pretty beat this afternoon."

Grace followed his line of sight and he saw her features turn down. "I'm going to take him into Holy Cross tomorrow morning. His energy level is dropping faster than it ever has before. Something's up with his blood-cell counts."

"We'll take it easy. Ride out onto the lower twenty and picnic under a scrub oak."

She nodded, but the worry lines around her beautiful blue eyes deepened exponentially, setting concern loose inside of him.

"We don't have to go today, Grace. We can put it off."

"Are you kidding?" She gestured toward Caleb. "He's been waiting for this all week. Sometimes I think the excitement of this adventure is the only thing keeping his spirit alive." She swallowed and a glimmer of tears flooded her eyes for an instant, before she blinked them back. "He's living one day at a time, so today he's going to live."

He reached for her and pulled her against him, feeling her body quake for a moment before she contained her emotions. By the time she stepped away she had a smile on her face.

"Come on. Let's go." She turned and jerked the tie on the reins, releasing them from the hitching post. "It's a beautiful day. I want to enjoy it."

Nick gathered his own tangled thoughts and untethered Jericho, anxious to channel the growing anger in his gut. He turned the bay toward Caleb and pulled him to a stop, staring down at the little boy who'd captured his heart and soul the first time he'd called him Mister Nick. He knew what he had to do. It wasn't going to be easy, but he'd do it anyway. He was choosing honor over duty.

"Ready to cowboy up, Caleb?"

Caleb grinned and rocked forward off the wooden railing he'd been sitting on. "Can we go fast?"

"Yeah. Today's the day you become a real cowboy just like Zachary-G."

He let out a whoop and scuffed his new boots in the loose Texas soil, stirring up a trail of dust behind him.

"Come on, let's ride." Nick scooped him up and put him in the saddle, then shoved his booted foot into the stirrup and swung up behind him. He wrapped his left arm around Caleb's chest to secure him and showed him how to lock his hands around the base of the saddle horn for stability.

Sometimes courage showed up in the most unexpected places, Nick realized as he turned his horse for the open landscape in front of them; and Caleb Marshall had plenty of it.

GRACE SQUINTED HER EYES against the afternoon sun filtering through the lacy branches of the scrub oak overhead, and leaned back into Nick's broad chest.

A steady breeze stirred in the range grass around them and ruffled Caleb's hair where he sat on the blanket they'd spread out under the tree, playing quietly with his toy horse.

Contentment seemed a strange companion at the

moment, but that didn't stop her from succumbing to it. Seeing her son grinning and laughing as Nick had loped his horse along had been therapeutic to them both.

"A penny for your thoughts," Nick whispered close to her ear.

"I haven't heard that phrase in so long. Where'd you hear it?"

"My parents used to say it to each other."

"It's sweet, but oblivious to the rising cost of living."

A deep chuckle resonated from his chest. "I'll go a buck."

"I was just enjoying this moment of peace. There haven't been very many of them for us lately."

He brushed his hand across the side of her head and worked his fingers into her hair. "Things will get better, Grace. I promise."

She closed her eyes to listen to the beat of his heart under her ear, and started when Caleb tapped her on the shoulder a moment later.

"Mommy. Wake up. I want to ride."

Dazed, Grace realized she must have dozed off for a second or two. It was no wonder, considering the amount of time she'd lain awake in Nick's arms last night.

Heat erupted on her cheeks as she sucked in a deep breath before leaning forward to stare up at Caleb.

"Where do you want to go?"

He turned and pointed to the massive barn several shallow rises away from their location. "I want to see the bats."

"There could be bats," Nick said from behind her, "and owls, and sparrows."

"Bats," Caleb repeated.

"I've been meaning to take a ride down there and

have a look around since we saw the flicker of light the other night. May as well be this afternoon. We're halfway there already."

"Are you sure?" Grace asked, turning to look at him, then back at Caleb.

"If he's up for it, so am I." Nick rocked forward onto his knees.

She studied her son, focusing on the tinge of healthy pink shading in his cheeks. "Then let's go."

Caleb bent down and picked up his bag of Goldfish, reached inside and pulled a couple out, then popped them into his mouth. "Now I'm ready," he said as he crunched them up.

Within a couple of minutes they'd broken down their picnic spot and Nick had everything stuffed into the saddlebags and tied onto the horse again.

He held on to Tulip's reins as Grace climbed aboard before he turned and picked Caleb up.

"You doing okay, bud?"

"I'm a cowboy now."

"Yes, you are. I'll have you pushing cattle before too long."

"Cattle?" Caleb asked, repeating the unfamiliar word.

"Cows. Moo. Cows."

Caleb nodded, understanding the bovine's call.

Nick lifted him up and settled him on the horse, then swung up onto the saddle behind him. After making sure Caleb had a good hold on the saddle horn, he turned Jericho and headed out for the old trestle barn, a relic that had been on the property for fifty years or more according to the locals.

He reined his horse in at an easy walk, enjoying his surroundings, while he contemplated his next move with the governor. He'd thought of little else since he'd made the decision to convince her to help her grandson, regardless of the consequences he could face. No secret was worth keeping if Caleb Marshall lost his life in the process.

"Does Bart Bellows own this land, as well?" Grace asked from next to him, their horses matching each other stride for stride.

"Yeah. Bought it for his son. Too bad he never came home from his tour in Iraq."

"That's sad," Grace said.

"Yes, it is." Nick couldn't keep thoughts of the men he'd lost there from invading his mind. Good soldiers who might still be alive if they hadn't listened to him. He gritted his teeth and turned his focus on the barn looming in the distance. He'd gained an ounce of peace with his past, thanks to Bart, who'd encouraged him to start over, to forgive himself and to find a path to redemption any way he could.

And maybe he had. Maybe the child in his arms was the way back.

Caleb pointed at the barn as they got closer. "It's giant, Mister Nick. Lots of room for bats."

Glancing over, he watched Grace make a face and shiver. "Let's hope not, Caleb. They carry rabies."

"What's a rabies?"

"It's not good, tiger. So if we see any bats flying around in broad daylight we're out of here. Understand?"

"Okay."

Just to be sure, Nick scanned the sky directly surrounding the barn, satisfied when the only winged creatures were half a dozen sparrows.

He reined in his horse just shy of the barn's two-story doors and dismounted, then gently lifted Caleb down from the saddle. Caleb took several steps back and craned his neck so he could see the entire face of the structure.

Nick caught him just before he tipped over. "Easy there." Concerned, he picked him up and held him in his arms so he could look up at the barn.

Grace stepped up next to them and touched Nick's arm. "I should have warned you, his condition can affect his equilibrium at times."

He nodded. "I'll watch him."

"Can we go inside?" Caleb asked, beginning to squirm in Nick's arms. "I wanna go in."

"Yeah, but you'll have to let me look first. Make sure there aren't any coyotes hiding out in there, or a skunk, or a raccoon."

Caleb's eyes went wild. He stopped fidgeting and stared at the doors with a measure of mistrust on his face.

"Skunks smell bad."

"Yes, they do, so stay with your mom and I'll have a look."

"Okay." Content to be on the outside for the moment, he didn't protest when Nick put him into his mother's open arms and headed for the massive double doors that had been barred with a wooden plank wedged into heavy metal brackets on either side.

Nick raised one end of the plank, popped it out of its bracket, then pulled the door open several feet and stepped into the cavernous barn.

Sunlight streamed in through the cracks in the structure's outer skin, highlighting billions of dust particles riding the shafts of light to the ground.

All clear—

A shrill scream sliced the air and brought Nick around.

"Grace!" he yelled, as a wave of panic drove him through the doorway and outside, where he spotted her stumbling backward from a massive clump of Texas sage less than thirty feet away, clutching Caleb in her arms.

He bolted toward them. Was something wrong with Caleb? He'd never forgive himself if anything happened to him.

Nick caught her from behind just before she went down hard, and lowered her to the ground in a sitting position.

"Grace! What's going on? Is he okay?"

Caleb pushed back and stared up at him wild-eyed and confused.

She nodded, sucking in deep gulps of air. "He needed a place to relieve himself. He said he couldn't hold it until we got home. I figured the bushes were good, but, Nick, there's someone in the brush."

Caution hissed across his nerves. Had the person who'd trespassed on the ranch several nights ago returned?

"I'll check it out." He came to his feet, reached back with his right hand, flipped the snap on his weapons holster and drew his pistol, glad he'd clipped it on his belt before they left the ranch. You never knew what kind of creatures you might encounter out here, including the two-legged kind with an agenda.

He moved forward, scanning for movement in the thick patch of Texas sage. Focused on the exact place he'd first spotted Grace and Caleb.

The impressions of her shoe prints were visible, and he followed them to the edge of the brush.

Nick came to a full stop and stared down at a familiar print pressed into the soil next to a pair of cowboy boots partially obscured in the tangle of branches and leaves. Careful to avoid the impression, he reached out, gathered a fist full of branches and pulled them back for confirmation.

"Damn," he whispered under his breath as he released the brush and holstered his pistol, going instead for the cell phone in his shirt pocket.

Unfortunately those boots were still on a man's feet. A man with a bullet hole drilled into his forehead.

Nick flipped open his phone and dialed 9-1-1.

Chapter Eleven

"You were right, Nick. It's a match to the boot impression we pulled over at the governor's ranch," Matteo said, holding out the casting he'd just helped Sheriff Hale's investigative team pour and lift.

Nick took it, staring at the distinctive sole pattern of the Marine Corps boot. "Whoever he is, he's probably the one who killed this guy. Could be our Wes Bradley."

Wade joined them and held up a plastic bag with a cell phone in it. "That's affirmative. Hale's forensic investigators found this buried in the straw in the barn along with signs that someone has been living inside. When I turned it on, I discovered its contact number matches the one we found on Trevor Lewis's phone for Wes Bradley."

"The kicker," Nick said, shaking his head in disgust, "is that the guy has been using my ranch house to shower and steal food. I discovered it yesterday, but I should have figured it out sooner."

"Don't be too hard on yourself, Nick," Matt said. "It's out of the norm for something like this to happen. A big, empty house, him in need of a place to hide—and don't forget, he was careful. Anyone of us could have missed the signs."

Harlan made his way over to the circle. "Hale found the guy's wallet intact, along with his driver's license. Guy's name is Joe Sims. He's a ranch hand at the Y-Bar-J next door. The foreman told Hale Sims went in search of his cow dog Wilson two nights ago. Wilson came home the next morning, but Joe didn't. He wasn't too concerned, since Sims had a couple of days off coming. He just figured the kid had taken off, until this morning, when he didn't show up at the ranch."

"He stumbled down here, right on top of our shooter, who couldn't risk having his hideout discovered, so he popped him and tried to stash his body." The summation was acidic in Nick's mouth, and he shook his head. "It fits. Two nights ago, I saw what looked like a lantern light. It was probably Sims's."

"Yeah," Wade said. "They found a Coleman lantern in the same area where they found the cell phone."

Nick looked up to where Nolan was deep in conversation with Sheriff Hale, no doubt relaying the information they had on Wes Bradley, sketchy as it was.

He slid his gaze to where Grace and Caleb were safely seated in the backseat of a patrol car, out of the mix of cops and bad news. Thankfully Caleb hadn't seen Sims's body hidden in the sagebrush, according to Grace, who'd blocked it from view.

"It looks like this guy is willing to kill anyone who gets in his way." Harlan rested his hands on his hips. "So you've gotta ask yourself, what's his next move? Who's his next target? What's his endgame?"

Nick's chest tightened as he contemplated the answers. "From what we've seen so far, he wants to take out the governor." His sense of duty amped up and he let his gaze lock on the patrol car where Grace and Caleb waited.

"Granted, she seems to be his number-one target," Harlan agreed.

"Hey, I've gotta take off, get them home. It's been a heck of a day, and Caleb's exhausted. I'll see you guys later. Let me know if Nolan plans a briefing." He stepped back and headed for the patrol unit, prepared to have Grace and Caleb driven back to the ranch house while he rode and ponied the other horse home.

One thing was certain—Lila Lockhart would be no good to Caleb Marshall if she died in an attack.

GRACE UNZIPPED the upper garment flap on her suitcase, reached in and pulled out the tattered manila envelope from inside. It represented the last barrier to the trust she knew had solidified between her and Nick; her trial transcripts. The events of that horrific night in her own words. Words she'd never bothered to read.

She took a peek at Caleb where he lay sound asleep in bed, flipped off the light switch and left the door open a crack so she'd hear him in case he woke up and called out for her.

Clutching the package to her chest, dressed in sweats and a T-shirt, she padded down the hallway barefoot and paused to stare into the living room where Nick sat on the sofa staring into the fireplace. She studied his handsome profile, strong jaw and straight nose. Maybe luck had finally found time to acknowledge her existence.

As if sensing her presence, he turned his head and looked at her, then reached out and patted the seat next to him. "How is he?"

She moved into the room, feeling the heat from the

flames in the hearth warm her skin. "Sleeping. It was an intense day for the little guy, but he came through it fine." Needing a measure of separation, she chose to sit down on the ottoman in front of him. "Thank God he only saw the man's boots and not his body. I'm not sure how I would have explained that to him."

Nick watched her with an intensity that made her heat on the inside, as well.

"What have you got there?" he asked, leaning forward to rest his elbows on his knees and lock his fingers together in front of him.

A flutter of doubt whispered through her, but she willed it away and gathered her fortitude. "I know you already know what happened in my past, but I want you to understand it from my perspective." She let go of the bulky envelope and held it out to him.

He took it from her and sat back, but his gaze never left her face. "What's this?"

"The trial transcripts. My testimony. The testimony my defense attorney says got me acquitted."

"And what do you think?"

Discomfort wiggled inside of her, but she met his gaze and contemplated his question. "I told the truth that day on the witness stand."

"But there's a part of you that still believes you committed a crime? Tell me, Grace. I want to hear it from your lips."

She blinked back hot tears that seemed to flame up from nowhere. She'd done everything she could to forget that night, and now the man she trusted, and cared for, was asking her to relive those horrific moments?

"I can't... I can't—"

"You have to." Nick tossed the package onto the

couch, reached out and took her hands in his. "I'm not going to judge your actions that night, Grace. Hell, I'm the last one who's capable of doing that. But I want the details to come from you. Then we never have to discuss it again. A wise man once told me, 'We're all human. We all make mistakes. Let's mitigate them and get on with living.' You can let go. You don't have to run anymore. That's what I want for you."

For us.

He pulled her into his arms, soothing her against him as he brushed his hand against her silky hair.

He stopped counting the minutes until she regained her composure, and instead tried to focus on his own dilemma, until she pushed back and looked at him.

"Troy Marshall hit me for the first time two days after I found out I was pregnant for the second time. I'd miscarried once before, and I used that fact to get him to stop, but I was terrified. I realized that I had to stay calm, or risk losing my second child. He didn't hit me again until Caleb was a year and a half old, not long after we learned he had aplastic anemia."

"Dear God." Nick reached for her and settled her next to him on the sofa. "I had no idea."

"I called the police and they sent his rookie-cop brother, Rodney, to escort him to jail for the night. The next morning he was apologetic and blamed his overwrought emotions on learning of Caleb's illness. Two months later, he did it again, and spent thirty days in jail before being released."

Nick swore under his breath as tension knotted his muscles. He'd have taken Troy Marshall apart if he wasn't already in his grave.

"At that point I asked him to move into the spare

room and I locked my bedroom door every night. He would bang on it and eventually go away, but one night he came home and flew into a rage outside of the door. I was terrified when he kicked it open and burst in. I could smell the alcohol on him. He hit me and blamed the sorry state of our marriage on Caleb."

"That SOB."

"Troy lunged for him, but I got to him first. He chased us to the top of the stairs." Grace sucked in a labored breath as he rubbed her hand where it lay in her lap. "And he grabbed for Caleb. I sidestepped Troy, spun around behind him and pushed him with my body in an attempt to protect Caleb. Troy lost his balance and went down the stairs headfirst. In an instant he was lying at the bottom in a heap. I called 9-1-1, but by the time they got there it was too late. Rodney Marshall showed up and called me a murderer. He was escorted away by his buddies, but not before he threatened to kill me over his brother's death."

"It wasn't your fault, Grace. You saved your child's life that night."

"A month later I was charged with manslaughter, and you know the rest." She let out one last stuttering breath and relaxed against him.

Nick continued to gently stroke her hair until he was certain she'd dozed off, glad he'd forced her to verbalize the details she'd refused to acknowledge for too long. She was finally free of her past.

Grace Marshall was free.

He watched flames reduce the logs to embers, then stood up, lifted her into his arms and carried her down the hallway to her room. As much as he needed to feel her next to him again tonight, he wanted her there of her own accord.

GRACE STEPPED OUT of the shower, toweled off and slipped on her clothes. Stepping to the vanity mirror, she took out the clip on her head and released the twist of hair she'd piled up to keep dry, shook it loose and finger-combed it.

If she'd known telling Nick about her past would have the cathartic effect last night's experience had, she would have done it sooner. Now she needed to thank him for pushing her to tell him what happened, because for the first time, she realized, she could see a future ahead for herself and Caleb.

Where was Caleb anyway? By this time on a Saturday morning he was usually up bouncing around and asking for a breakfast pancake shaped like a cowboy boot, but he'd still been asleep when she'd headed into the bathroom half an hour ago.

Maybe he'd found Nick in the kitchen and put in his request by now.

Grace flipped off the light, pulled open the door and stepped out into the bedroom.

Concern glided across her nerves as her gaze settled on the bed and Caleb's tiny form still snuggled up on his side under the covers.

"Caleb?" She moved toward him. "Hey, sleepyhead, it's time to get up." Sitting down on the edge of the bed next to him, she brushed the top of his head, smiling at the down-soft feel of his blond mop of hair. "Caleb?"

He didn't respond, no movement, not even an attempt to open his eyelids.

She shook his shoulder. "Caleb!"

Panic zipped through her system as she pulled the covers down and rolled him onto his back to make sure he was breathing.

She shook him again. "Caleb! Wake up! Please wake up!"

No response.

Terror cut away the last of her composure.

"Help! Nick!"

Grace's terrified scream echoed through the house and slammed against his eardrums like a hammer. He dropped the spoon he'd just used to stir his coffee and bolted out of the kitchen.

In a matter of seconds he was in the bedroom where Grace worked frantically to wake Caleb up. He went to his knees next to the bed. Assessing the rag-doll consistency of Caleb's tiny body and the lack of color in his skin.

"He won't wake up, Nick. I can't get him to wake up." Grace turned a pleading blue stare on him that ripped his heart apart.

"I'm calling an ambulance." He pulled his cell out of his pocket and dialed 9-1-1 before searching for Caleb's pulse, unsatisfied until he felt it drum under his fingertips at the child's carotid artery.

"Hang on, buddy. Help's on the way."

"You need to take this, Grace," Dr. Cal Murphy said, holding out a slender black case.

Nick watched her reach for it, pull back, then finally complete the task reluctantly.

"Caleb is going to need a complete transfusion twice a week now of red cells, white cells and platelets. His stem-cell levels of production have dropped. I've requested that he be moved up the transplant list for the best human leukocyte antigen match we can find to avoid post-transplant rejection complications."

"And the transfusions, will they still allow him to function like a normal little boy?"

"Within reason, Grace, but I'd like to see him try to conserve his energy as much as possible. No rough play, to prevent bruising."

She nodded and leaned back into Nick; he responded by putting his arm around her waist and pulling her closer, trying to give her the support he knew she needed right now.

"I'll send the Donor Coordinator, Melissa Johnson, up to give you the particulars on the protocol if the beeper goes off, but be aware you'll need to come to the hospital immediately so Caleb can be flown to the donor's location."

Nick didn't like the look of grim determination pulling Dr. Murphy's brows together.

This was bad. Caleb's condition was deteriorating at a pace that scared the hell out of him. He could only imagine what it was doing to Grace.

"Hang in there, Grace. We'll find a suitable donor match." Dr. Murphy patted her shoulder, and glanced into the room where Caleb was. "You can take him home in an hour or so. By tomorrow, he'll be back to his normal self, and we'll transfuse him again on Tuesday. I'll get it scheduled with my nurse."

Grace nodded, snagging hope from the optimistic grin that flashed across the doctor's mouth.

"We'll be here." She watched him turn and hurry down the corridor of the pediatrics unit, bound for his next emergency.

Reluctant to remove herself from Nick's reassuring hold on her, she turned in his arms instead, and faced him.

"Welcome to my world," she whispered as he pressed a kiss onto her forehead.

"You're a trooper, Grace, and he's your copilot." Nick canted his head toward the bed where Caleb played with a couple of toys. "I don't have a clue what Doc Murphy just said. My reaction to a fight has always been to come out swinging and ask questions later."

"Our approach isn't that much different." She pulled back and stepped through the doorway into the room. "I ask questions first, then come out swinging."

He followed her in and stood at the end of Caleb's bed. "Looks like that ride yesterday whipped ya."

Caleb grinned. "Nope. It's my sick. My counts was low."

Grace listened to her son try to explain something most four-year-olds knew nothing about, and smiled in amusement. He was doing pretty well, staring up at Nick, and her heart squeezed in her chest.

"I got three—" he used his left hand to hold down the thumb and pinkie on his right hand, then held up three fingers "—kinds of things in my blood. Red cells, white cells and dinner-plates."

"Huh," Nick said, watching him with a serious expression Grace could see was about to crack. "Do you mean platelets?"

Caleb nodded vigorously. "Yep, and you got them, too, Mister Nick."

"I sure do, buddy. And I'd give them to you if we matched."

Caleb grinned and settled back against the pillows behind him. "We match," he said. "See?" Fingering up a piece of his hair, he worked it in between his little fingers.

Nick's cell phone vibrated inside his shirt pocket, but he ignored it, waiting for Caleb to finish.

"The same color," he said, as he let out a sigh then slowly closed his eyes.

"Take your call, Nick," Grace whispered. "He'll be out for a while."

He nodded, unable to swallow the lump in his throat as he fished the cell phone out of his shirt pocket and stepped out into the corridor, where he looked at the phone screen.

The Corps Security and Investigations headquarters number came up on the caller ID. No doubt Nolan had put together a briefing on yesterday's events at the ranch.

The call rolled over to voice mail and Nick headed for the waiting room to pick up the information, finding an unoccupied corner, where he entered his access code and listened to Nolan's message that a mini-briefing would start in half an hour. He closed the phone and headed back to tell Grace he'd be back for her and Caleb within the hour. They would be safe at Holy Cross until he returned.

"COFFEE?" AMELIA OFFERED as she carried the serving pitcher around the main open area of CSaI headquarters.

"No, thanks," Nick said. "I'm too wound already." Leaning back on his desk, he studied the other team members.

She moved on and filled Nolan's cup again.

"The coroner confirmed that Joe Sims's time of death was Wednesday night, sometime between 7:00 p.m. and midnight."

Nick nodded. "Around 8:00 p.m. is when I caught sight of the flicker of light from my kitchen window."

"Prelim on the weapon used, a 9-mm pistol," Wade said, stepping forward. "And I got a call last night from my buddy in the Marine Corps death-notification office that Wes Bradley was confirmed dead, and identified through dental records. Whoever is roaming Freedom using his name isn't the real Wesley James Bradley."

"Anything on a list of soldiers in his unit?"

"Negative. Won't come in until the end of next week, Nolan."

"Dammit. And Governor Lockhart isn't backing down from her press conference at Cradles to Crayons. Looks like we need to ramp up the security to make sure she's safe. Matteo and Harlan, put together a diagram of the location and a one-hundred-yard perimeter. I'll talk to Sheriff Hale and see if we can request some additional law-enforcement officers from surrounding counties to cover the outside venue. The governor will call in her personal protection detail from Austin, as well."

"Nick, how much longer are you on assignment for the governor?"

"I'm not sure, Nolan, but I can warm a chair inside."

"Good. Everyone else is to do the same. You're to monitor everyone who comes into the room, and escort anyone out who looks or acts suspicious. We still have a slick shooter out there somewhere."

Nick tried to relax, but his nerves were frayed. He was going to get his chance to speak with Lila Lockhart at the event. His one opportunity to change her mind, and save Caleb Marshall's life.

Chapter Twelve

"Order up," Valerio Rodriguez said, putting a couple of plates of food along with their order ticket up on the pass-through window ledge.

Grace looked at the ticket, pulled the plates and headed for table number five.

"Meat loaf, baked potato?" she asked at the booth where a nice older couple sat.

The gentleman nodded, and she slid his meal in front of him, then served the corned-beef Reuben to his wife.

"Can I get you folks anything else?"

"No, miss. Everything looks great."

"Enjoy your supper." She smiled, put the ticket face-down on the table and headed for the counter, where Faith was waiting.

"So, how's it going?" Faith asked as she topped off a couple of water glasses with a pitcher.

"Rather well, I think. It's amazing how easy it was to get back into the flow of being a waitress. I'd forgotten how much I enjoy it."

"Good. I'm glad you're here."

The front door opened, triggering its distinctive little bell jingle. Grace glanced up to see Stacy and Zachary Giordano walk into the café. Stacy spotted her, and clutching Zachary's hand, headed straight for her.

"Grace, I'm so glad to see you. I was sick when I heard you'd taken a leave of absence from the preschool. Not to mention how much Zachary misses Caleb. How is he doing?"

"You're both welcome to check for yourselves. He's upstairs in Faith's apartment with Nick, a sitter and Kaleigh."

"Grace, why don't you take your break and go up for a visit? I can handle things down here until you get back."

She turned a grateful smile on Faith Scott, a woman she already knew was becoming a friend. "Fifteen minutes?"

Faith nodded.

Grace untied her apron and put it under the counter, then went around to where Stacy and Zachary stood. Zachary was busy trying to separate his hand from his mother's, but she was having none of it.

"Bailey told me you were going to be working at Talk of the Town a couple evenings a week. I'm just glad I picked the right one."

"Me, too." She showed them to the stairs leading up into the apartment. "Caleb misses Zachary, too, and he's got a couple of new adventures to tell him about."

Stacy chuckled. "Maybe we better plan them a play-date. I haven't got all night."

"Let's do that." Grace stopped on the landing and knocked on the door, which immediately opened, and she found herself looking at Nick. Her heart rate kicked up as she studied him in the backlight.

"Zachary-G and Stacy stopped by for a visit. The boys miss each other."

"Come in. You're just in time to help us put a puzzle together."

Zachary finally obtained his freedom from the mother ship, and he hurried into the apartment. A moment later, he and Caleb were galloping toy horses and chattering.

"Thank you, Grace. For letting them see each other. Zachary has been a little hard to handle lately. Even Charlotte Manning commented on his sullen demeanor this morning."

"Oh, Stacy. I'm so sorry. I had no idea. But until something changes for the better with Caleb's health, it's just too risky for him to attend right now."

"But you are coming to the governor's press conference on Thursday, aren't you?"

"Yes."

"Oh, good. Bailey mentioned that she'd called you, and you'd agreed to attend. Let's make sure the boys get to sit together."

"Let's do that. I'm slated to be in the second row with my students. Zachary is welcome to take the chair next to Caleb."

"And I'll sit directly behind him, to make sure he stays put," Stacy added as she eyed her little boy.

Warning bells went off inside Nick's head as he listened with growing concern to Grace and Stacy's exchange. It had been foolhardy to believe that just because Grace had taken a leave of absence, she wouldn't attend the event. She was, after all, a preschool teacher whose students would benefit from the new program the governor planned to announce.

Nick gritted his teeth and tried to put a semipositive

spin on the ever-developing situation. Maybe having Grace and Caleb there was just what he needed to convince the governor to change her mind about the transplant. To finally put a face on the very one who needed her help the most of all right now.

Every muscle in his body pulled tight, the tension crushing him in a viselike grip that wouldn't release. His only hope was that he'd be able to keep them all safe from a crazed killer with his crosshairs on Governor Lila Lockhart...

And any collateral damage that happened to be standing too close to her at the moment he decided to strike.

NICK GLANCED into the classroom as it filled with preschool students and their parents.

Bart Bellows was in the process of parking his electric wheelchair in the back corner of the room, with the assistance of his medical attendant, Roger Adams, a burly guy capable of physically lifting Bart whenever necessary.

Notes of music being played by the high-school band drifted in through the open doors as their version of "Hail to the Chief" echoed from outside in the parking lot.

Half the town of Freedom appeared to have shown up already, and the event wasn't scheduled to begin for another half hour.

Everyone seemed to be in a festive mood, and happy about the governor's announcement—everyone except the CSaI team members wandering around, watching for anyone who might try to hurt the people they cared for. Still, he couldn't help but notice he hadn't seen Lindsay Kemp, or her and Wade's twins, Lacey and Lyric.

If only he'd have been able to convince Grace and Caleb to stay home, as well. Though Grace had considered his request, she'd ultimately decided to come, citing her admiration for Governor Lockhart and her respect for Bailey.

Blood really was thicker than water, even if she had no idea they were her mother and half sister.

He sucked in a breath and turned back into the hallway, spotting Governor Lockhart through the panel of glass in the security door leading out to the playground area of Cradles to Crayons. He watched her makeup artist, Becky Davis, dab her face with a makeup sponge and go over her lipstick with a brush.

This was his one chance, and he might not get another anytime soon. Hell, he wasn't even certain he'd be able to return to CSaI after he'd said his piece.

Determined, Nick walked across the corridor, pulled open the door and stepped inside, just as Becky finished up and stepped out, leaving Nick and Governor Lockhart alone together.

GRACE TOOK THE STEPS up to the main entrance of Cradles to Crayons clutching Caleb, and stepped well into the corridor lined with book nooks and coat hooks before she put him down.

An armed officer stood at the threshold out into the main hallway. She took Caleb's hand and approached him.

"Officer."

"Howdy, miss. What's your name?"

"Grace Marshall, and this is my son, Caleb Marshall."

He casually scanned the clipboard he held. "There

you are. Take a left once you're in the hall. The classroom will be immediately on your left."

"Thank you." She smiled and nodded even though she didn't need directions.

The officer stepped aside to let her pass and waited for the next person behind her to approach.

Glancing up at the security door directly across from the main entrance, she caught a glimpse of Nick on the other side in a heated discussion with someone she couldn't see.

A little buzz of excitement worked through her body, leaving her limbs tingling. She'd fallen for him. Her heart knew it, her mind knew it, and her body knew it, too. Had from the first time he'd touched her.

Caleb must have seen him, too, because he jerked his hand free of her grasp and bolted for the door.

"Mister Nick!" he yelled, banging his hand on the door once before she could reach him and pull him back.

Grace knelt in front of her son. "Caleb, Nick's speaking with someone right now. It's rude to disturb him. We'll see him after the governor gives her speech. Okay?"

"All right." Caleb dug the toe of his right boot into the tile, his mouth pulled down in disappointment.

"Put a smile on and cowboy up. You get to sit next to Zachary-G."

In less than a second, he was grinning, and she rose to her feet just as Nick moved slightly to the side, revealing the person he was speaking with in the hallway beside him.

Governor Lila Lockhart—and she wasn't happy, judging by the firm set of her jaw.

"Come on, sweetheart, let's get to our seats." Con-

cerned, Grace quickly took Caleb's hand and headed
for the classroom, wondering what on earth she'd just
witnessed, but once they entered the classroom, her curiosity evaporated, replaced by the palpable excitement
of the parents and students waiting for the governor's
entrance.

Freedom, Texas, was proud of its own native daughter.

Grace focused on her seat on the end of the second
row and smiled at Stacy Giordano where she sat in the
third row directly behind Zachary.

"Here, Caleb." She pointed to the chair next to Zachary and stepped in next to her son to take her seat. Immediately, the two boys' heads tucked in a conspiratorial
bow, as they each pulled out their favorite toy horse for
a competitive gallop.

The feel of a familiar hand on her shoulder brought
her head around, and she stared up for a moment into
Nick's steel-blue eyes. "Hey."

"Hey, yourself," he mouthed over the hum in the
room, then bent toward her ear. "I'll meet you out by
the Tahoe at the conclusion."

She nodded, missing his nearness the moment he
straightened and worked his way to the back of the room,
where he joined several other men she recognized from
Corps Security and Investigations.

Bailey Lockhart stepped to the podium at the front of
the classroom and a whisper of shushes passed between
parents and their children, until the room had quieted as
much as possible for a passel of excited four-year-olds.

Even Caleb and Zachary reined in their horses long
enough to look up at Miss Lockhart.

"Good afternoon, students and families," she said into

the microphone. "And welcome to Cradles to Crayons. This afternoon I have the pleasure of introducing you to my mom."

A round of applause broke out in the room as Governor Lila Lockhart stepped through the entrance into the classroom and made her way to the podium where she stopped next to her daughter.

"The governor of the great state of Texas, and the next president of the United States of America, Lila Lockhart!"

Emotion closed Grace's throat as she clapped so hard her fingers stung. Caught up in the excitement, she looked directly at the governor, and found her staring back with an odd look of interest furrowing her forehead and narrowing the space between her sky-blue eyes.

Time seemed to move at half speed as she retrained her stare on Caleb for half a second before Bailey hugged her and surrendered the podium.

Taken back by the exchange, Grace pulled in several deep breaths and straightened in her seat. Perhaps Nick had told the governor just how sick Caleb was in an effort to plead that the sealed adoption records be opened. She was the most powerful woman in Texas at the moment.

Nick shifted uncomfortably on his feet as he watched the exchange transpire between Grace and Lila, wondering if he'd gone too far, but knowing he hadn't gone nearly far enough in convincing her to help her grandson.

The clapping died down and the governor started her speech.

"Since I was a child, I've loved a good book. It didn't matter who read the words to me before I could read, or who turned the pages, I enjoyed the story. So today I'm proud to announce my early-reading program, See Me Read. A community grant program that will involve local libraries, school libraries, community centers, parents, grandparents and siblings. A city- and town-wide effort to share the written word with every child and tap into the vast store of folks in our communities who would love to share their time and effort to help beginning readers learn—"

Sheriff Hale stepped into the room and headed straight for Governor Lockhart with two deputies hot on his heels.

In less than five seconds, she'd been escorted out of the room.

Nolan's finger went to his earpiece, and a hush fell on the crowd as Hale grabbed the microphone.

"Everyone, stay calm. There has been a bomb threat called in to our dispatch center. I need y'all to file out of the room in an orderly evacuation of the building. We've got a five-minute window."

The hair on the back of Nick's neck prickled.

Agitated, he turned to where attendant Roger Adams was already helping Bart Bellows get his wheelchair turned and pointed in the right direction, but as he looked out over the crowd, he could see panic starting to build.

Mothers grabbed their children and pulled them onto their laps. Fathers bolted up from their seats.

Two seconds later, the earsplitting whine of the school's tornado siren violated the air, and pandemonium erupted as all hell broke loose in the crowded classroom.

Nick sucked up against the wall to avoid being

stepped on in the ensuing crush to get out. Worried, he tried to pick out the exact spot where Grace and Caleb had been sitting near one of the doors, and caught sight of the top of Caleb's head as he filtered through the opening with Zachary and several others, then vanished into the hallway.

Where was Grace?

In under two minutes the stampede was over, and Nick surveyed the chaotic scene in front of him.

"Nick! Over here," Wade hollered, as he knelt next to an elderly gentleman who'd been knocked down. Charging over, he helped get the man up, and Wade put his arm over his shoulder, wrapped his other around the man's waist and headed for the door.

Matteo was busy scooping up a little girl who was holding her arm, and Harlan was clearing a pile of overturned chairs out of the path of Bart's wheelchair.

Scanning the debris, Nick spotted something, then prayed to God he was wrong. The end of the pink scarf Grace had been wearing.

Panic drove him forward, as he tossed kiddy chairs like Tinkertoys, and found her in almost the exact spot she'd been sitting.

"Grace!"

She rolled over and sat up. "Once I was down, I couldn't get up. Where's Caleb?"

Nick helped her to her feet and followed the last person out of the room, Nolan, carrying a little boy whose face was tear streaked as he cried for his mother.

"I saw him zip out the door with one of the first waves. He's gotta be in the parking lot right now with Zachary Giordano."

"Thank God," she whispered as she leaned against him. "I can't believe how fast that went bad."

They hurried through the main door and headed for the back of the parking lot where everyone stood, staring at the building in a state of shock.

Grace's heart threatened to pound out of her chest as she scanned the crowd, trying to remember exactly what Caleb had on, but for the life of her, she couldn't think.

"Do you see him, Nick?" she pleaded, finally spotting Zachary standing next to his mother, Stacy, but no sign of Caleb.

Hopeful, she hurried toward them. "Stacy, do you know where Caleb is?"

"No. He came through the class door with us, but I don't recall seeing him after that."

Grace went to her knees, reached out and touched Zachary's arm. "Zachary. Do you know where Caleb is? Did you see which way he went?"

Slowly, Zachary raised his arm and pointed his index finger at the building.

Horrified, Grace turned to stare at Cradles to Crayons. "Oh, dear God. The tornado siren. The storm cellar. He's in the storm cellar."

Panic invaded her cells, shooting adrenaline into her system. She bolted, focusing on the building as she dodged a couple of officers who tried to stop her.

Behind her she heard the sound of Nick's voice calling her back, but it was quickly drowned out by the blare of the tornado siren. As much as she cared for Nick and trusted his judgment, she loved her son and could never let anything happen to him if it was in her power to stop it.

Nick got within a hairbreadth of Grace, but missed his tackle as she took the steps faster than him and ran into the preschool.

"Grace! Wait!"

Heart pounding, he rushed down the hallway and out into the main corridor, where he slid to a stop. Storm cellar. Where in the hell was the storm cellar?

The pounding of footstep on stairs brought his head around to the right. Less than twenty feet down the hall, he spotted a door ajar several inches, and sprinted for it.

He pulled it open just in time to see a flash of blond hair at the bottom. "Grace!" Hell, their five minutes was almost up according to his internal clock. Any second now he expected to be blown to bits, but he couldn't let that happen to Grace and Caleb.

Pounding down the stairs behind her in the eerie emergency lighting, Nick took the corner and stared at the big empty room, and the storm cellar at the far end, where he could clearly see Grace on her knees in front of Caleb.

"Grace! Let's get out of here."

Nick took three steps forward and stopped.

Turning slightly, he stared in disbelief at the open wire grate under the stairwell.

At the red digital clock ticking off the seconds in tiny red numbers.

10...9...8...7...6...

Bolting for the tornado shelter, he burst through the door and pushed it closed behind him, hearing the latch lock into place.

3...2...1...

The explosion rocked Cradles to Crayons.

Chapter Thirteen

Nick slowly raised his head but kept his hold on Grace and Caleb from behind their makeshift barricade, a pallet of water bottles.

Overhead, the emergency lighting continued to shine and a fresh-air-ventilation fan kicked on behind a small grate in the ceiling.

"Are you both okay?" he asked, stepping back to visually check them over.

"Yes," Grace whispered as she smoothed her hand along Caleb's cheek. "What happened, Nick?"

"The bomb was planted under the stairwell. I just happened to see it, but by then it was too late to do anything but get inside the shelter before it detonated."

"I never expected to have to use it after all the tornado drills we've practiced down here, but it saved our lives." She blinked and looked around. "What do you suppose it looks like outside?"

Nick pulled in a breath. "Don't know. But fortunately everyone got out of the building in time."

"They probably think we're dead."

"It's a good bet." He pressed a kiss onto her forehead, and caught Caleb staring up at them. Nick squatted down to look him in the eyes. "You doing okay, Caleb?"

"I didn't like that big noise." His chin started to quiver and the first sign of tears illuminated his wide blue eyes.

"Neither did I, buddy. But we're okay. Not a scratch on us."

Caleb nodded, and Nick put his hand on the child's shoulder. "I'm going to get us out of here."

Caleb lunged forward and threw his arms around Nick's neck. He reciprocated and gathered the little guy up, feeling his tiny body tremble. "Don't be afraid. Just start thinking about the story you'll have to tell Zachary-G."

The diversionary tactic seemed to work and he felt Caleb relax in his arms. Nick hugged him tighter, then released him and came to his feet.

"Stay here next to your mom. I'm going to see if I can get the door open."

Grace pulled Caleb back against her. "Be careful, Nick."

He turned for the heavy blast door that had been built to withstand a tornado's direct hit. The latch was intact, a good sign, but it didn't mean it hadn't been compromised on the outside, or that there wasn't a ton of debris piled up in front of it on the other side.

Nick gritted his teeth, grasped the latch handle and jerked it. It jammed the first try, but on the second pull it released.

Easing it open a crack, he smelled the air coming in for smoke, but only a hint lingered. A good sign that the bomb's blast percussion had snuffed out most of the flames. They wouldn't be walking into a wall of heat.

"No fire," he said over his shoulder to Grace as he strained to swing the door open wider against some resistance.

Staring out into the dust-filled air, he could see the stairway they'd used to come down no longer existed. It had been annihilated in the explosion, but the sound of sirens echoed through the gaping hole it had once occupied.

He looked back at Grace. "Stay put. I'm going to see if I can get someone's attention."

"Okay." She gave him a reassuring smile.

Turning, he slipped through the gap, and scrambled over a two-foot-high pile of twisted debris that had been blown against the door.

Nick could hear the sound of voices above him.

Hurdling the last obstacle in his path, he got as close as he could to the opening.

"Help! Down here! Help us!" He listened for a response, then shouted again.

"Nick!"

"Harlan! We're down here. In the storm cellar!" He picked his way closer to the opening, climbing over the debris field blocking his path.

"Harlan!"

"I can hear you, Nick! The fire department is on its way. They'll get you out. Hang on."

Relief surged inside of him and he sat back onto a piece of debris he was sure had once been a stair tread. They'd been seconds from death. Reality pushed the air out of his lungs in a long, steady whoosh.

Times were, he'd gotten a rush out of a scrape with disaster, but he now knew his internal landscape had changed. Emotionally, he knew why.

He'd fallen for Grace and Caleb Marshall. There was no going back.

He didn't want to.

GRACE PULLED THE BLANKET an EMT had given her a little tighter around her body and tried to follow the man's instructions.

"I'm going to shine a penlight in your eyes. Stare straight at it."

"Okay." She pulled in a breath and stared into the light.

"Pupils equal and reactive." Another EMT nearby scribbled the information down on a run sheet.

"You're sure you weren't struck by any flying debris?"

"Positive." For added emphasis, she smiled. "Now I'd like to hold my son."

"Go ahead." The medical technician stepped aside and she climbed into the back of the ambulance where Caleb sat on a gurney having the same series of tests.

"He looks great, Miss Marshall. You really lucked out getting into that shelter when you did."

"Yes, we did." She glanced up at Nick where he sat on a padded bench that ran along the opposite side of the compartment. They'd lucked out all right. If Nick hadn't spotted the bomb, and closed them in the shelter when he did, the outcome would have been grim.

Looking out through the back doors of the emergency vehicle she was struck by the chaos in the parking lot.

Five additional ambulances had arrived at the scene and were in the process of treating those who'd been cut by flying glass when the windows in the preschool blew out.

"Sign here, Miss Marshall, and you're both free to go."

Grace took the clipboard and scribbled her name.

Begrudgingly she unpeeled the blanket from around her shoulders and surrendered it.

"You're welcome to exit through the side door." The EMT reached over, popped the latch and pushed the narrow door open.

They climbed out onto the asphalt and Grace wobbled slightly trying to find her balance.

Nick steadied her. "Stay here. I'll go for the Tahoe," he offered.

"Okay. That'll give me a minute to get my legs underneath me."

He brushed her arm with his hand and took off across the parking lot.

Grace leaned against the side of the vehicle and sucked in deep gulps of air in an attempt to calm herself.

Caleb pressed against her side and she gently cupped his head to her body and closed her eyes.

It was a miracle no one had died.

"You are not fine, Mother." The sound of Bailey Lockhart's voice brought Grace's eyes open.

"Will you please have a look at her. She's bleeding from her arm."

"Calm down, Bailey, it's only a scratch," Lila said, but there was an edge of concern in her voice.

"Governor Lockhart, let me take a look."

Grace recognized the voice of the EMT who'd checked her pupils with his penlight.

"It doesn't hurt," Governor Lockhart insisted. "Well, maybe a little."

"Mom! That's a lot of blood."

"Chambers, grab a pressure dressing ASAP! Governor, you need to sit down."

"It was such a tiny piece of glass," she reasoned.

Grace's heart rate spiked up. Was Governor Lila Lockhart going to be okay?

"It was big enough to cut into your brachial artery, Governor. We're going to need to get you to the hospital stat. What's your blood type?"

"Oh, you're not going to find much of it here, but I periodically donate it to myself so there'll be a supply if I need it—"

"She has a rare blood type. She's AB negative," Bailey half said, half yelled.

"Oh, dear God," Grace whispered, feeling her knees go limp as she slowly slid down the side of the ambulance and collapsed on the asphalt.

Was it possible? Was Governor Lila Lockhart her birth mother?

And before that thought even had time to register, another one entered her brain. Nick had been speaking to the governor, arguing with her before the event... Had Nick known the truth all along?

But...she'd trusted him....

Grace's insides imploded, crushing her heart like an eggshell.

"Chambers, make the call to medical control, have them type and cross-match five units of AB negative stat from anywhere they can locate it."

"Momma." Caleb reached out and patted her on the head. "What's wrong?"

Grace stared up at her son through a screen of blistering tears.

It explained the argument she'd seen Nick having with the governor less than an hour ago. It explained the odd look the governor had given her from the podium before her speech, and the way she'd looked at Caleb.

Her grandson, Caleb, who needed her help.

The family resemblances they shared.

The fact that Bailey Lockhart was her half sister, and she hadn't known.

Her horror reached a crescendo, evaporated and turned to anger. She wiped her tears, scrambled to her feet, took Caleb's hand and struck out across the parking lot to find a ride home.

NICK MADE A SECOND LAP around the Cradles to Crayons parking lot and finally approached Stacy Giordano, who was having a cut on her arm looked at.

"Hey, Stacy. You haven't seen Grace and Caleb have you?"

"They're gone."

"Gone? To the hospital?"

"No. I saw them get into Faith Scott's car five minutes ago."

Worry arced over his nerves, and he stared at the spot where the ambulance had been minutes earlier. "Someone get transported?"

"You didn't know? Governor Lockhart got hit by a piece of glass in the upper arm. Apparently it hit an artery. Bailey said they need to get the bleeding stopped, and she needs blood or she could die. She has a rare type. I never knew that. Bailey just told me."

Nick swallowed as he put the gut-twisting scenario together in his head. "Did Grace approach from over there?" He indicated the spot where the emergency vehicle had been parked.

"Yes. I saw her standing next to it when they took the governor over to be examined…and, Nick, she'd been crying."

"Thanks, Stacy. Glad you and Zachary are okay."

"Me, too. Take care of yourself."

He turned his back and headed for the Tahoe, then spotted Nolan waving frantically from a huddle of uniforms and the other members of the CSaI team.

"What the…"

"Nick!" Nolan hollered, coaxing him over with his hand.

"Hey, buddy, you all right? You don't look so good." Concern affixed itself to Nolan's face.

"I'm fine," he lied.

"Nick, Bart's missing, along with his black van. A couple of deputies just found Roger Adams's body on the other side of the building with a couple of bullets in his head."

"Have you tried to raise Bart on his cell?"

"Yeah. He's not picking up, but Sheriff Hale is issuing an APB for his van right now."

Nick brushed his hand over his head and tried to pull himself together.

Grace and Caleb were gone.

Bart Bellows—his friend and mentor—was gone. His assistant had been murdered.

Nick's heart squeezed in his chest as he fell back on his military training.

"What do you need, Nolan?"

"I'm calling an emergency briefing in half an hour. We've got to figure out why Bart was the target, and who took him."

"I'll be there."

Nolan slapped him on the shoulder as he turned to leave.

He'd be there all right, since his current assignment had just ended and taken his heart with her.

"THESE ARE COPIES of Bart's declassified CIA files, and his personal information. Take a look at them, see if anything pops." Nolan passed out the folders marked Confidential across the front in bold red letters.

"Did the APB produce any hits on Bart's van?" Matteo asked from across the conference table.

"Negative. Odds are whoever took him is holed up somewhere. He's not stupid. He knows to lie low until the heat dies down," Nolan offered.

"But we're not going to let that happen, are we?" Harlan added with determination.

"For country, for brotherhood, for love," Nick intoned.

A round of agreement went around the table as each team member sounded off on the CSaI motto.

"We'll get him back," Nolan promised, but every man in the room knew that possibility diminished with each passing hour.

"Sheriff Hale has put an alert on all of Bart's accounts if a transaction takes place. We can do our part by tearing into these files."

Nick opened the folder and splayed the paperwork in front of him, scanning for anything that might explain why Bart had been kidnapped, but the case information was antiquated.

Next he scanned the stack of personal information that belonged to Bart, a task that bothered his sense of right, until he hit on information about Bart's son.

"I knew Bart had a son. Says here his name's Victor. He was declared MIA in Iraq five years ago."

"That's a long time to be gone," Wade mused.

"I agree. But what are the odds he's still alive?" Nick wondered out loud.

"Bart told me he did an extensive search for Victor immediately after he was reported missing." Nolan shifted in his chair. "Even used his CIA contacts, but they didn't turn up anything. There were rumors that he'd been taken by the insurgency and transported into Afghanistan. No doubt the enemy knew his daddy was worth big bucks, but Bart said he never received a ransom demand of any kind."

"The kid's probably dead," Harlan speculated. "Buried in some godforsaken hole in the sandbox."

"He was a handful," Matteo said as he tapped the file in front of him. "Had more than his share of run-ins with the law from the time he hit puberty."

Nick shook his head in wonder. "Auto theft, shoplifting, armed battery. How does that happen? Bart certainly would have given the kid anything he wanted. Why'd he believe he needed to steal it? Makes no sense."

"Troubled. He was a troubled kid." Wade shook his head. "Makes me want to go home and hug my girls."

"Odds are Victor Bellows is dead and there have been no reported sightings of him for five years." Nolan rocked forward in his chair and studied the team. "What we need to do is try to make some sort of connection between Bart's kidnapping and Governor Lockhart. Is there any way these two events are connected?"

"Could be," Harlan said. "If the anarchist group who bombed the first fundraiser also bombed the preschool today—"

"What the hell for?" Nick asked. "So the governor can't implement a program to help early readers?"

"Nick's right. The motivation just isn't there. There wasn't a single nut job from that group in the crowd. They weren't even in town. I think the explosion was a simple diversion so he could kidnap Bart. We were so busy believing that the governor was the target, we failed to think outside the box," Matteo said, before shaking his head in disgust.

"As much as I hate to swallow that assessment, Matt," Nolan said, "you could be right. Maybe Bart was the target all along. He's been by the governor's side from the beginning. He was at every event where an attack transpired."

A tense hush fell on the room and Nick knew each man was considering the implications of missing the identity of a true target. Being duped had a rancid flavor that lingered in the back of his throat.

"Let's adjourn for the evening, head home and get some sleep. I want everyone back here at 0800 hours. Maybe we'll have some news by then. Dismissed. Oh, and you'll have to leave the files here at headquarters. We can't risk having any information leak out, not even via a casual glance by a loved one."

Each man put their copy of the confidential folder on the pile as they filed out of the conference room.

Nick paused next to Nolan. "Where's Parker tonight?"

"Holy Cross with the governor and her family."

"How's she doing?"

"Great. They did minor surgery and closed up the tear in her brachial artery before the bleeding got out of control. They're going to keep her until tomorrow afternoon."

"Glad to hear it." Nick tossed his file on top of the heap, and turned to leave.

"Oh, hell, I just about forgot. Parker phoned right before the briefing. The governor wants to speak with you tomorrow morning at 0900 hours in her room at Holy Cross. I'm going to assume it's in regards to your assignment for her."

"Of that, I'm certain. Good night, sir." He left the conference room and headed home, mentally preparing for what he would find when he arrived.

He wasn't disappointed.

Standing with his shoulder pressed against the jamb of Grace and Caleb's empty room, he stared at the made-up bed for longer than was healthy. They'd no doubt gone back to Grace's condo. His only consolation was that Rodney Marshall had probably left town and was no longer a threat to them, but he'd continue to keep watch.

He loved them…and he'd lost them.

Could he ever get them back?

GRACE TOPPED OFF Deputy Jeff Appleton's coffee cup and cleared away the dessert plate he'd scraped clean of Faith's cherry pie.

"Thanks, Grace."

"You're welcome."

At the other end of the counter, Faith Scott and Stacy Giordano chatted over an issue of a bridal magazine.

The dinner crowd was thinning out, and Grace paused long enough to grab a glass of water.

"Hey, Grace, come here." Faith motioned her over. "We need your expert opinion."

"Which bridal bouquet do you like best?" Stacy asked, turning the glossy magazine toward her.

"Hmm." Grace studied the two bouquets of beautiful

flowers and settled on the hot-pink gerbera daisies over the hand-tied red roses. "The roses would be beautiful for a Valentine's Day wedding, but I like the daisies, because they're so happy."

"Those are what I picked." Faith looked at her and smiled. "I know it's short notice, Grace, but I'd like to invite you to my wedding, that is, our wedding. Matt and me. It's Sunday afternoon at 2:00 p.m., at the little white chapel on the edge of town. Do you know it?"

"Yes." Touched, Grace hugged Faith. "I'd love to come. Congratulations. Matt is a lucky man."

"He is, isn't he?" Faith said, grinning. "So, Stacy, out with your news."

Grace felt the tingle of excitement in the air as they simultaneously drew closer together, perhaps so every patron in the café didn't hear.

"I'm pregnant. I found out this morning, and Harlan and I are celebrating with a date night tonight."

"Congratulations," Grace whispered, glancing around to see if anyone else had overheard the exciting news, but the remaining customers in Talk of the Town were busy working on their dinner plates instead of their eavesdropping skills.

"We're planning a New Year's Eve wedding, and praying that Bart will be home safe and sound by then."

Faith shook her head. "Just awful what happened yesterday at Cradles to Crayons. I'm so thankful I didn't take baby Kaleigh with me, or go inside that classroom. Matteo said utter chaos broke out. We could have been crushed."

Grace couldn't keep a shudder from rocking her body as she remembered the scene with vivid clarity, including someone's foot in the middle of her back.

Stacy noticed and patted her hand. "I'm so glad you all made it out alive."

"Me, too." Choked up, Grace excused herself, and made busy filling napkin holders with her back to the restaurant while she worked to get her emotions under control.

The tragedies of yesterday went far beyond near death and broken glass. They cut straight to her heart with scalpel-like precision.

The bell over the café door jingled. Not unusual, but it was the determined stride of cowboy boots across the tile floor that she recognized. Her breath caught in her lungs. It was a sound she'd come to anticipate, only because it belonged to a man she'd trusted and cared for.

Without turning to verify what she already knew, she looked at Faith instead. "Mind if I take my break now?"

"No, go ahead. It's long overdue."

"Thanks." She untied her apron strings on the way into the kitchen, and hung it on the coatrack next to the back door on her way outside into the alleyway behind the establishment.

She couldn't avoid Nick indefinitely, not unless she skipped town, but she wasn't sure she was prepared to go toe-to-toe with him, either. Her emotions were still too raw.

"Grace."

His voice on the air behind her was like a long-distance caress. She closed her eyes for an instant against its effect, then turned to face him.

"You lied to me by omission, Nick. I trusted you, Caleb trusted you, to help us, and you knew the entire time she was my birth mother, and you—" Grace's throat closed, but she fought the crushing restriction and refocused her rant.

"Don't worry. Your mission was a total success. I've got no intention of contacting her, blackmailing her or whatever the hell you believed I was capable of. A match for Caleb will come. I just have to believe it will happen or I'll lose my—"

"Good God, Grace." In three strides he was there, pulling her against his chest.

She settled for a moment, sucking in the strength and security that was Nick Cavanaugh, then she severed the connection and jerked away.

"I never want to see you again." She hurried in the back entrance of the café and closed the door behind her. Now she was the one who'd lied.

Nick didn't try to follow her.

Everything she said was true. He'd known from the beginning of his assignment that it could end badly, and he'd been willing to accept the collateral damage then; but not anymore.

He headed for the Tahoe, planning the biggest reconnaissance mission of his life.

Chapter Fourteen

Grace rolled over and attempted to stuff her head under her pillow, but the rhythm of the jarring recoil on the bed next to her convinced her escape was impossible...or maybe it was Caleb's giggle combined with an infernal beeping noise.

Jolting awake, she sat up and watched him take another leap into the air as he bounced up and down on her bed, holding the pager the hospital had given them in his clinched hand.

A bleating beeper.

"Good morning, Caleb. Give Mommy the beeper."

"Seat drop," he yelled, kicking his legs forward and landing squarely on his bottom. "Here." Hand outstretched, he opened his fist.

Grace's heart rate picked up as she took it like a nugget of gold and turned the tiny viewing screen so she could read it.

Holy Cross Hospital.

Excitement churned in her veins. "Hurry, little man. Get dressed. We've got to go to the hospital right away."

"I don't wanna go there anymore." His mouth turned down.

She reached out and pulled him to her, settling him

on her lap. "The wait is almost over, sweetheart." She stroked his hair and gazed into his big blue eyes. "Someone has decided to give their bone marrow to you, Caleb. This will be your most important adventure ever. What do you say? Can you cowboy up for Mommy?"

"Yeah." A weak little smile turned his mouth, and she hugged him to her before letting him climb down onto the floor next to the bed.

"Now get dressed. We need to get going."

NICK PACED THE HALLWAY outside transplant coordinator Melissa Johnson's office, waiting for Grace and Caleb to step off the elevator and come down the corridor.

Hours of negotiations with Governor Lockhart had taken a toll on his brain, but he knew they'd turned a corner this morning when her test results had come in, and a match was made.

Grace could hate him for the rest of her life, but he could sleep at night now, knowing he'd taken a stand on the side of honor.

The sound of little bootsteps pounding in the hallway brought his attention around, and he watched Grace and Caleb come in his direction.

Caleb spotted him first. "Mister Nick!" he shouted, as he bolted forward before Grace could catch hold of him.

Nick's throat tightened. Putting his focus on Caleb, and not on the look of anguish on Grace's beautiful face, he scooped him up unto his arms.

"How are you, buddy? You feeling okay these days?"

"Yep. Where's your horse?"

"At home in the pasture."

"Can I go there, to see him?"

"Caleb," Grace scolded.

"It's okay." He stared at her, trying to read her body language, trying to gauge where she stood as far as he was concerned, but he got nothing.

"They'd like you inside." He motioned to the coordinator's office door. "Governor Lockhart is waiting with the news you've been anticipating."

Gratitude washed across her features, but she masked it in a matter of seconds. "I suppose I have you to thank for this?"

"I may have had something to do with it, but in the end it was her decision. She wants to see you, Grace."

Her eyes watered for a moment, and a hint of a smile materialized on her lips.

"Caleb is scheduled for his transfusion down in the first-floor pediatric ward in ten minutes. I'll have to take him down first, so they can get started."

"I'll take him down," Nick offered, watching a brief look of uncertainty set a crease between her brows before it relented.

"Nurse Brinkley handles his prep. He likes her best. She's so gentle with him that—"

"Go inside, Grace. I've got him."

"Thank you," she whispered before she turned, opened the office door and went in.

Battling an ache in his chest the size of a small country, Nick headed for the pediatric ward with Caleb in his arms, but he wanted Grace there, as well.

GRACE'S NERVES TWISTED into a knot as she stared at the tough-looking two-man security detail standing outside the door of Melissa Johnson's office.

The waiting area had two more men in suits sitting

at attention in chairs on either side of the room, and the assistant who normally worked behind the desk greeting people wasn't present today.

Governor Lila Lockhart was important, and Grace couldn't even begin to imagine what it took to keep her safe, but she did know that she risked a media blitz if word leaked out. This all had to be part of her strategy to assure she controlled the news cycle.

"Miss Marshall." An official-looking gentleman wearing a black suit and an earpiece stepped out of Melissa Johnson's office and approached her.

"I'm Jim Scarborough, Governor Lockhart's chief of security when she's in Austin." He reached out and she shook his hand.

"Come with me."

She followed him through the door leading into the interior office, an office she'd been in two dozen times since moving to Freedom, but she found it almost impossible to focus on the familiar setting when Lila Lockhart was the woman behind the desk today.

"Governor," Jim said, pausing next to the door while he motioned Grace deeper into the room.

"I'd like total privacy with Miss Marshall, Agent."

"Certainly. I'll be right outside." The agent left the room, pulling the door shut behind him.

"Please sit down, Grace," Lila said in an official tone suitable to her position.

Heart pounding, Grace was grateful to make contact with the padded seat of the chair in front of the desk before her legs wobbled out from underneath her. "Thank you, Governor."

Palpable tension excited the molecules in the air

around them and forced her stomach into a tight knot she could feel clinch inside her.

"First let me start by saying you have a beautiful son."

Grateful for the verbal opening, she felt some of the choking tension inside of her release its grip.

"Yes, he is. His name's Caleb."

"CSaI Agent Nick Cavanaugh told me all about him, in the vein of a proud father."

Grace's heart squeezed in her chest. "He's very fond of Caleb, and Caleb's fond of him."

"Cavanaugh has been very persuasive. I'm not a heartless woman, but we must necessarily deal with this entire situation very carefully. I've got my trusted media team working on a solution, and I need to speak with my family."

Grace met the governor's intense gaze and watched her smile through a veil of tears, as her official persona dissolved like chalk in the rain.

"I've often wondered about you, child, since the morning I let them take you from my arms. I was young and foolish, and believed myself to be in love with your father, who's gone now. But my family would have none of it. They'd already planned my entire future. Tell me, Grace, did you have a good childhood? Were your parents kind and loving to you?"

Lila inched her hand across the desk, and Grace pushed forward in her chair. Through a blanket of tears, she grasped her mother's fingers, as the dam broke on Lila's emotions and her clear blue eyes loaded with moisture.

"Yes. They were wonderful to me. I always knew I was loved."

"You're a beautiful young woman, Grace. Can you ever forgive me for letting you go?"

"I already have." It wasn't enough for her to hold her mother's hand any longer.

She stood up and hurried around the desk to meet Lila on the other side, where they fell into each other's arms.

GRACE SHIFTED IN HER SEAT, the third pew from the back of the packed church, glancing around at all the people who had come to witness Faith and Matteo's marriage.

Half the town of Freedom by the looks of it. Her sense of community swelled and she realized that this was her home, too.

On the opposite side of the aisle, one row in front of her, she'd spotted him. The neat clip of his hairline across the back of his neck. The crisp white of his dress shirt against the fading tan of his complexion. If she closed her eyes and conjured it, she could even smell the male scent of his skin, spicy and warm.

A surge of longing battered her emotions and sent a wave of heat through her body. She swallowed and diverted her gaze, only for it to return to him, and find him staring back.

Nick Cavanaugh had come through for Caleb, and for her in the end. She just wished she could find a way past the feelings of betrayal resonating inside of her.

He broke the visual connection first and turned to face forward, as the first notes of the bridal march echoed from the piano at the front of the church, and everyone rose to their feet for the bride's procession.

Grace pulled in an excited breath and focused on Faith as she made her way up the aisle. She looked charming in her grandmother's antique wedding gown and veil. She'd contributed to Faith's traditional something borrowed, and loaned her the diamond earrings left to her by her adoptive mother.

Joyous tears welled in Grace's eyes. Faith had found happiness with a man she loved, and they would raise baby Kaleigh together.

There were great things in life, and she was thankful they'd found them.

At the head of the aisle, Faith paused, and Matteo reached for her. She hooked her hand in the crook of his arm. Then together they took two steps forward together and stopped in front of the minister.

"Please be seated."

A collective whisper of movement filled the candlelit church as everyone settled into their seats.

"We are gathered here today to unite Faith and Matteo in the bonds of holy matrimony."

Grace tried to still the workings of her mind as she listened to the minister's words, but it was impossible. The phrases—in sickness and in health, for richer or for poorer—applied to her and Nick. Hadn't he cared for her and Caleb in all of those circumstances? Hadn't he provided her with all those things that Faith and Matteo were pledging to one another right now? Hadn't he proven he was a good man, who loved honor?

Her heart squeezed in her chest as the reality of her feelings for him solidified. She loved him, in spite of the secrets he'd withheld from her, and Caleb loved him, too.

Blinking back tears, she glanced his way and found him looking back at her with a grin on his lips.

She smiled back.

Perhaps she would stay for the reception after all.

It was a place to start.

"ALL UNITS. UNIT ONE, please respond to a stolen-vehicle sighting at milepost 117, Highway 83 northbound. I'm in pursuit of a black van, tag number BELLOWS, for failure to stop."

"Copy that, Unit One. Unit Five en route, southbound at milepost 109. I'll deploy spike strips."

"Affirmative, Unit Five. Go ahead. Our ETA is eight minutes to your location."

Nick stepped down on the gas pedal of his pickup and broke the boundary of Freedom proper, as Nolan reached and turned up the volume on the police scanner from his shotgun position in the passenger seat.

Fortunately Sheriff Hale had spotted Bart's stolen van twenty minutes earlier and the chase was on when the driver of the vehicle refused to pull over.

"Looks like Sheriff Hale plans to put the squeeze on him, sir."

"Let's hope he doesn't find a way to slip through the noose. This guy's a slippery bastard."

Glancing up into his rearview mirror, he focused on Harlan and Wade in the Tahoe behind them. The entire team wanted in on the takedown, save Parker, who was behind locked doors with the governor and her family right now, learning that they had an illegitimate sister; someone they knew. Matteo was absent, too, because he was spending a couple of days away with his new bride, Faith.

Nick's gut pulled taut as he considered the dangers of a high-speed chase. Especially one with Corps Security and Investigations founder Bart Bellows strapped in a wheelchair in the back.

Gritting his teeth, he pushed down on the accelerator, determined to get there as fast as he could.

With good police work, Hale would nab the man who'd taken Bart before he had a chance to escape, and solve the mystery of who'd executed the attacks against Governor Lockhart, along with committing three murders, all in one fell swoop.

It was a lot to hope for, but he did it anyway. Anxious to see Wes Bradley, aka unknown, take a hard fall.

Nick caught the flash of emergency lights in his side mirror and eased over to let a responding patrol car fly past. Glancing at his speedometer he clocked the guy at 70 mph and saw his brake lights come on.

"Oh, hell, would you look at that," Nolan said from next to him, as he leaned forward to stare out the windshield at the chaos two hundred yards in front of them.

He let off the accelerator and the pickup slowed before he applied the brakes, flipped on his blinker, eased over onto the shoulder, stopped and turned on his hazard flashers.

The dust was just beginning to settle a hundred yards up the strip of asphalt as they climbed out of the vehicle and were immediately joined by Wade and Harlan.

"This doesn't look good," Wade said from next to him.

"Not if he hit that spike strip doin' ninety." Nick knew blown tires could send a rig haywire, and Bart's van was top-heavy.

The wail of another siren blared behind them as they broke into a jog on the side of the highway, and an ambulance rolled past.

Had Bart been injured in the crash, or worse?

Nick couldn't keep his pace from stepping up, but he wasn't alone, as his fellow team members sprinted next to him.

They all cared about the man who'd seen something in each of them that they hadn't been able to see in themselves. They all loved Bart Bellows like a father.

Nick focused on the path of a set of black skid marks carved into the asphalt at the point the van's tires had exploded on the spike strip. The van had careened across the center line and disappeared over the edge of the roadway, down into the deep borrow pit on the opposite side of the highway.

"Oh, no," Nick said as they all four pulled up short in the loose gravel on the side of the road and stared at Bart's crushed van. It had obviously rolled several times before slamming into the earth.

One by one they shuffled down the steep embankment and rushed to the crash scene, where Sheriff Hale was busy handcuffing a scruffy-looking kid with a bleeding gash across his forehead before turning him over to EMS.

He was no Wes Bradley, hell, far from it, but he'd been behind the wheel of Bart's van.

"I'm sorry, boys," Hale said, shaking his head.

Nick held his breath, dreading the Sheriff's next words as if he knew what every one of them were.

The crash had been violent. What were the odds Bart had survived?

"Bart Bellows isn't inside, gentlemen. His wheelchair's locked in place, but he's not there."

Relief shattered Nick's nerves, but just to be certain, he hustled to the pile of wreckage that had once been a state-of-the-art vehicle, squatted down and stared in through one of the shattered rear windows.

Bart's power-driven wheelchair was still locked in place in its track system, designed to keep the chair stationary during travel.

Nolan was beside him in an instant, followed by Wade and Harlan, all determined to confirm the fact for themselves.

"What's that?" Nick pointed to a bead of moisture balling on the downhill side of the black leather chair seat and oozing out of a crease in the padding.

In slow motion he watched the droplet collect, then break free and drop to where it spattered against the inside panel of the van, revealing its composition.

"Get Sheriff Hale," Nick said, glancing back at the team and feeling his caution level raise. "This entire wreck is a crime scene. That's blood."

Harlan turned and headed for the sheriff, with Wade on his heels. In a matter of seconds, Hale joined them, staring in at the ever-growing pool of dark red blood that oozed from Bart's wheelchair.

"I'll be damned. I'll get the forensics team out here before we flip this rig back up onto its wheels."

"What did the driver have to say?" Nolan asked, staring back to where the kid sat handcuffed to a gurney.

"He claims some guy gave him five hundred bucks to get in the van and drive north on 83 like he stole it. Says he gave him another five hundred to outrun any law-enforcement officer who tried to stop him."

"Can we question him?" Wade asked, working the knuckles on his right hand with his left.

"Now keep your cool, Mr. Coltrane. I know this kid. He's a local, been in plenty of trouble, but he'll give me a good description. He took a heavy-duty bump on the head in that crash."

"Relax, Wade," Nolan advised. "We know this fits Wes Bradley's M.O. He's a master at diversionary tactics. He's got Bart and they're probably halfway to hell and gone by now."

Nick hated to think of Bart Bellows in that situation. Bleeding and helpless without his wheelchair. Subject to a madman's terror. They had to find him—before it was too late. And judging by the amount of blood dripping off of Bart's wheelchair, that was already a possibility they had to consider.

Chapter Fifteen

The mood in the conference room was somber, as each member of the team stared at the Texas highway map Nolan had rolled out and affixed to the wall the moment they'd made it back to CSaI headquarters.

"We know the Highway 83 incident was a diversionary tactic to throw us off the scent. My guess is Wes Bradley headed east or west on 287, or went north and picked up Interstate 40."

Concern adhered to Nick's insides as he studied Nolan. He was making himself sick over Bart's disappearance. Hell, they were all upset, but it wouldn't make Bart Bellows suddenly appear in the room.

"Did the kid give any indication that he knew what kind of vehicle the guy was driving?" Wade asked, then added, "I'd have liked to beat it out of him."

Harlan nodded. "Me too, but Bradley doesn't make very many mistakes."

"Sheriff Hale is dusting the entire van for prints. Maybe we'll get something to go on. In the meantime, I'd like to spearhead the investigation and search for Bart. I owe him..." Nolan's voice broke. He cleared his throat and continued. "My life."

"We're all beholden to him, Nolan, in one way or

another, but you know as well as we do that Bart wanted you in D.C. personally taking care of Governor Lockhart's first national fundraiser. He didn't want it any other way." Nick finished saying his piece and glanced around the table at his fellow team members, who were nodding in agreement.

Nolan raked his hand over his head a couple of times, before looking up at them. "You're right." He nodded several times in agreement, but Nick could see that he was upset.

"You'll have to excuse me for a moment." Nolan left the conference room and seconds later they heard his office door close in the outer loft.

Wade cut loose a low whistle. "What was that about?"

"Don't know," Nick said, "but he wasn't happy when he got home from D.C. last time. Claims it's too cold."

A hush fell on the group as each man considered the myriad of reasons for Nolan's odd reaction.

"I'm going to head down to the station, see if Sheriff Hale has gotten anything usable out of the kid yet." Nick stood up. "I'll give you a call if there's anything we can use." He headed out of the conference room, determined to find something, anything that would point them in the right direction. But dead ends were the most likely scenario if history repeated itself where Wes Bradley was concerned.

Unfortunately, there wasn't a single thing he could do about it.

Nick walked through the main entrance and hustled down the stairs to the lower level of the building, wondering how Grace's meeting with Lila Lockhart had gone. He would most likely see her tomorrow at the community Thanksgiving luncheon, since he'd promised Lindsay Kemp he'd attend.

In the section of the structure that housed a massive garage, he couldn't help but glance up at Bart's extra van parked in the far corner. Bellows was a bit of a mystery, but he'd always been good to his team.

Jumping into his pickup, he fired the engine and triggered the main exit door.

If he were Wes Bradley, why in the hell would he kidnap Bart Bellows? Nick ruminated on the question as he shifted into Drive and pulled around, heading toward the exit. Bellows's past was ancient history; it was hard to find a grudge in the files they'd poured over.

He and the governor appeared to have been friends for half a century. Maybe he'd been taken to try to collect a ransom from her sizable fortune. He nixed that idea, since Bart could outspend her by a hundred to one.

Turning the wheel, he pulled through the overhead door and slowly rolled out onto the gravel driveway.

If they could isolate a motive, they could dial in on a suspect.

Nick felt his pickup come off its wheels half a second before he heard the explosion.

A fireball was the last thing he saw rolling over the hood of the truck.

GRACE'S CELL PHONE rang just as she finished buckling Caleb into his car seat for their short trip to Holy Cross. Tuesdays and Saturdays were his treatment days, and she was counting the minutes until the transfusions were no longer necessary. Until Lila gave him the gift of a new life.

"Hello?"

"Grace?"

"Stacy. Hi. How are you?"

"I'm fine, but I just got off the phone with Harlan. There's been an explosion outside CSaI headquarters."

She sucked in a quick breath as a sense of worry settled over her. "Is everyone all right?"

The pause was telling. "Stacy? Is everyone okay?"

"Nick hit an IED with his pickup, Grace. They're taking him to Holy Cross right now—"

Grace closed her phone, climbed behind the wheel and sped off for the hospital.

"HOW MANY FINGERS am I holding up?"

Nick tried to focus as the fuzzy image blurred then came together in front of his face.

"Three."

"You've sustained a mild concussion, Mr. Cavanaugh. It should heal on its own, but you'll need to take it easy for the next week or so, and I'd like to keep you overnight for observation."

He thumped the soft cast on his left arm that went from his elbow to his wrist. "How long do I need to wear this thing? Eight weeks?"

"Maybe longer. We'll reassess it in the morning after the swelling goes down, then put it in a solid cast." The E.R. doctor stepped toward the privacy curtain. "You've got visitors. I'll send them in."

"Thanks." Nick leaned his head back against the pillow and closed his eyes. Who knew he'd hit a blasted IED on U.S. soil instead of in Iraq? It had destroyed his pickup—he loved that truck—but at least it hadn't destroyed him, thanks to the quick thinking of his CSaI brothers upstairs. They'd pulled him out to safety before the entire rig went up in flames.

Opening his eyes, he focused on Caleb and his double as he lifted the curtain and ducked under.

"Hey, bud."

"Mister Nick, you are hurt." Caleb came up to the side of the bed and brushed his tiny hand over the cast on Nick's arm. "Are you gonna be okay?"

"You know it." Blinking hard, he pulled Caleb into focus, and watched Grace slide the curtain aside and step in to join them.

"Hey, soldier." She eased onto the foot of the bed, reached out and rubbed her hand on his lower leg. A warm sensation spread though his body like quicksilver.

"Nice gown," she said. "But I don't like the way you got it."

"Yeah, I can think of better things to wear, or not."

Their gazes met and Grace wet her lips. Maybe it was the IV pain meds dripping into his system, but he suddenly felt goofy all over.

"Caleb has his transfusion in ten minutes. I'm so thankful you're okay. Get some rest."

"I'd like that." He studied her, wishing he could reach out and trace the side of her face with his fingertips, but he was getting sleepier with each passing second. He closed his eyes for a minute, but when he opened them again, she was gone.

Unconsciousness was bliss, Nick decided as he stared at his team members gathered at the foot of his hospital bed.

"You did it, buddy. You caught us the break we needed. We just scanned the security-camera footage from outside the main garage door, and caught an image of the guy burying the IED in the driveway," Nolan said. "He matched Wes Bradley in build, and better yet, we got a brief shot of the vehicle he jumped into, a full-size pickup with a topper. The kid who crashed Bart's van remembered seeing a similar vehicle near where he met with the man, and he described him as having the same build, even thought he spoke to him wearing a ski mask."

"We got the vehicle description to Sheriff Hale. He issued a statewide APB. If Bradley is still in Texas, we're going to find him, and Bart," Wade added.

Nick's head throbbed. He glanced at the window to try to gauge the time of day, then closed his eyes.

"Get some rest, Nick. You deserve it after what just happened. We'll be back in the morning to pick you up." Nolan's voice blitzed through his mind, then peace descended around him as the room cleared, leaving him to dream about the woman he so desperately wanted to hold right now.

"I NEED A BROKEN ARM, so I can have that much pumpkin pie," Matteo joked as he stared across the table at Nick.

Grace laughed as she looked at the gathering of CSaI men and their loved ones around the large table on the edge of the community-center floor, where Freedom's townsfolk enjoyed a Thanksgiving luncheon organized by Lindsay Kemp, complete with turkey, mashed potatoes, stuffing, cranberry sauce, green beans, hot rolls and plenty of pumpkin pie with whipped cream.

"Great job, Faith," Stacy said as she forked another piece of Faith's pumpkin pie and put it in her mouth.

"Grace helped me with most of it."

"Um, I rolled the crust." She glanced over at Nick, who sat on her left.

"Every little bit helps," Lindsay said as she bobbed her gaze between Grace and Nick, as if she were trying to figure out just how they fit together in the relationship department.

Grace glanced over and caught Bailey staring at her with a sweet smile on her face.

They shared a secret the entire state of Texas would know about in a few days, when Governor Lockhart went before the cameras to tell her story. They were friends and half sisters; Grace couldn't be happier... unless...

"How's the cleanup going at Cradles to Crayons?" she asked Bailey.

"Good, now that the ATF has finished sifting through the remains of the storm-cellar stairs. I've got a crew set to replace the windows starting on Monday, then another one goes to work on the inside around the first of December. We should be able to reopen by the first of the year."

"Great news."

"You will be coming back to teach, won't you?"

Grace nodded. "Of course. I'll be there."

"Good, because we miss you. I miss you."

"Thanks." She almost said "sister," but clamped down on the word before it could escape.

Nolan Law began tapping his butter knife on his glass and got everyone's attention, including the children at the kids' table right next to theirs. He picked up his glass of juice and raised it.

"I'd like to propose a toast of gratitude to each and every one of you, and tell you how thankful I am to know you, to work with you and to have you as my brothers. To Corps Security and Investigations, and to the safe return of our mentor, Bart."

Everyone raised their glass. "Cheers."

The toast was made, and Grace couldn't help but notice each man's mood. She couldn't blame them for being down. Their boss was missing. The heart of their organization. And the circumstances couldn't be grimmer.

"So, how are you feeling, Nick?" Faith asked from her seat at the table directly across from them, where she gently rocked baby Kaleigh in her arms.

"Not too bad. They put a permanent cast on this morning, and I occasionally see double, but it's clearing up. I'll be 110 percent in a week."

"That's good news."

Nick's cell phone vibrated in his shirt pocket. Anxious, he pulled it out with his right hand and stared at the number. "Sheriff Hale," he announced to the team members as he pushed back his chair and headed for a quiet corner in the community center.

"Cavanaugh," he answered.

"I heard about the IED you hit, son. I sent for the ATF to look into it, along with the bombing at Cradles to Crayons. Turns out they found some of the same components at both scenes."

Nick digested the information. "Any news on the truck he was driving?"

"Negative. We've advanced the APB into neighboring states."

"Thanks, Sheriff. You ought to consider getting down here to the community center before the food's all gone."

"Thank you. I just might do that. Bye now." Hale

hung up and Nick closed his phone single-handed and slipped it into his pocket.

"Any news?" Nolan asked from behind him.

Nick turned around and found the rest of the team there, as well. "Nothing on the vehicle, but Hale extended the APB into the surrounding states. He also called in the ATF on both of the bombs, and found out they're linked by components."

"Damn," Wade said, "this guy's one crazy SOB."

"All we can do is stay alert." Nolan added. "Protect our loved ones."

Nick watched Grace come to her feet, pick up her purse, loop it over her shoulder and retrieve Caleb from the kid's table.

"I've gotta run, but keep me posted if anything else comes up."

"You do the same," Nolan said.

"Hey, Nick, wait up." Parker charged after him.

"Tell Grace the governor has scheduled the press conference for the day after Thanksgiving, at the Twin Harts Ranch, 11:00 a.m. You might want to bring her out and look after her. It's going to be chaotic for her and Caleb once the press sets their sights on them."

"Copy that, buddy. Thanks for the heads-up."

"You're welcome."

Chapter Sixteen

Nick took off to catch Grace, making it to her and Caleb just before she unlocked her car.

"Grace."

"Yes." She turned to look up at him.

"I need to talk to you. Can I follow you back to the condo?"

She hesitated, then seemed to relent. "Yeah."

Reaching down, he stroked the top of Caleb's head, then headed for the Tahoe, his ride until he bought a new pickup.

Grace adjusted her rearview mirror and focused on Nick behind her. Her heart was beating fast, her nerves were frayed, and she was bubbling inside like an excited schoolgirl who'd just been asked out by the best-looking boy on campus.

She loved Nick with every cell in her body, and she planned to tell him this afternoon.

Nick glanced around the condo, taking in the taste of its new flavor. Grace had put a couple pictures on one wall in the living room, and decorative pillows on the sofa. There were even a couple family photos sitting on the shelf above the TV.

It had a homey feel to it now, as if she were living there for the very first time.

"Coffee's on," she said from the kitchen.

He broke off staring at the pictures he was certain were of her adoptive parents and headed for the bar that separated the kitchen from the dining room. "I like what you've done in here."

"Me, too. It was about time I settled in, put down roots, if you can do that in a rental."

The sound of Caleb making his horse whinny at the top of his lungs from inside his bedroom caused them both to chuckle.

"I've got to help him work on that," Nick whispered as he moved closer to her. "I've got to work on a lot of things that are important to me."

She stared up at him and swallowed. Her eyes were bright in the overhead lighting, and he could almost feel anticipation and promise in the air around them.

"I realize you're still upset that I withheld information, but I'd do it again out of a sense of duty. You have to understand that I was caught between a rock and a hard place. My duties at CSaI had to come first...and then I met you and Caleb." Emotion squeezed his throat closed when he thought about the little boy who'd stolen his heart, right along with his beautiful mother.

"Come back to me, Grace. I'm a better man when you're in my life."

"Yes," she whispered, stepping forward to press her hand against his cheek. "You're all about honor, and doing what's right, Nick, and I love you."

Reaching out with his good arm, he cupped her chin in his fingers and raised her mouth to his.

Contact. Sweet, mind-blowing contact enhanced by

the emotional bond that had just been verbally established between them. It anchored him to the spot and made the kiss that much sweeter, but he couldn't deny the fire that licked through his body as he released her chin and wrapped his arm around her. He pulled her as close as he could while he explored her willing mouth.

An intake of breath, followed by the sound of Caleb's boot soles on the floor next to them, broke the kiss.

They both turned to look down at him and the funny way he puckered his lips into a perfect O shape.

"Kissing," he said. "Zachary-G told me 'bout that. He said his mom is kissing Mister Harlan all the time."

"Did he now." Nick sobered and tried to look serious, even though he could feel Grace quaking with silent laughter. "I'm thinking you're going to have to get used to seeing it, Caleb, because your mom and I, well, we like each other. A lot," he added, watching Caleb wrinkle his face up as he thought about it for a moment.

"Okay." A huge grin spread on Caleb's face, and he hopped a couple of times before turning and heading into the hallway. "Baby. Baby. Baby. Baby. Baby." The words drifted off as he skipped through the doorway of his bedroom.

"I guess you haven't heard." Grace looked up at him. "Stacy Giordano is expecting. Mister Harlan is going to be a daddy. Zachary is going to get a baby brother or sister next year."

"How great is that," he whispered, looking at her. "Harlan McClain joins the Daddy Corps ranks for a second round. I'll have to congratulate him the next time I see him."

"Yes, you will." Grace took Nick's right hand and

pulled him into the living room, where they sat down on the couch facing each other.

"How'd it go with the governor the other day at the hospital?" he asked, curious to know if her expectations had been met, if she'd managed to cut through the wall of resistance that was Lila Lockhart.

"We talked for hours. She wanted to know everything about me, about my childhood and my adult life."

"Everything?"

"If you mean my past in Montana, I told her about that, too. She didn't bat an eye. Said right is right, and there's nothing that can stand in the way of the truth. She's going to make a fabulous president."

Nick reached out and brushed his hand along her arm. "Come home with me, Grace. You and Caleb, today, right now. I don't want to spend another night without you."

"I can't. Not yet. Not until the coming firestorm settles."

"Parker says Lila has scheduled the press conference for the day after tomorrow, 11:00 a.m. at the Twin Harts Ranch. He advised me to drive you out there and provide protection."

"Is that really necessary?"

"I think so. They want to control the news cycle. It's a huge story, with the potential to derail her presidential bid. They're going to put the best spin on it they can, but the press can be aggressive."

"Now Caleb and I are just a news story?"

He saw a look of hurt invade her blue eyes, and he squeezed her hand. "Lila cares about you, Grace. Don't forget that fact when she puts her political face on."

"I'll try not to."

Nick's cell phone went off in his shirt pocket. He fingered it out with one hand and Grace helped him flip it open.

"Hello."

"Nick?"

"Oh, hey, Nolan, what's up?" He pushed forward on the couch, feeling the first charge of concern jolt through him.

"I just got a call from Sheriff Hale. The APB produced a hit on an abandoned vehicle an officer flagged, ten miles west of the Oklahoma state line."

Nick held his breath, praying that they'd found Bart, as well, injured but alive. "Did they find him?" He felt Grace's hand brush against his back in a gesture of support, and closed his eyes for a moment.

"The pickup was empty. The trail's gone cold."

"Damn." Nick pulled in a breath and released it through his teeth. "Thanks for the call. Something's going to come up."

"Yeah. I'm going to head down to the conference room to try to make myself useful. Talk to you later."

The line went dead and Nick closed his phone, then dropped it into his pocket before settling back on the sofa.

"Bart?"

"They found the pickup, but nothing else. No driver, no Bart Bellows."

"That at least means he's still out there somewhere. You can pull a measure of hope from that, can't you?"

He gazed at her, lost for a second in his desire to hold her again, but he needed to get moving. "I suppose I have to."

Fatigue and worry combined in his bloodstream to

give him an overwhelming sense of loss where Bart was concerned. Unfortunately he knew the entire team at CSaI was feeling the same kind of helplessness.

"I've gotta get over to headquarters. Nolan is there pounding his head against this thing, and I can't let him do it alone."

"I understand," she said, pushing up from the couch. "But promise me you'll take it easy. You still have a concussion."

"I will." He stood up. "Caleb," he called, and smiled when Caleb hurried out into the living room to see him.

"Yeah."

"I'm taking off, buddy."

Caleb wrapped his arms around Nick's legs and squeezed him.

He brushed the top of his head and told him goodbye.

"See ya, Mister Nick." He hurried back to his room.

Grace walked with him to the front door of the condo. "I'm preparing Thanksgiving dinner tomorrow night around seven. Will you come and join us?"

"I'd like that." He brushed a kiss on her lips, opened the front door and headed out.

GRACE HUMMED ALONG with the soft-music CD she'd popped into the player while she worked around the kitchen preparing Thanksgiving dinner.

The yummy smell of rosemary herb-rubbed turkey baking in the oven made her mouth water, and she hoped Nick would like it as much as she did.

She'd put Caleb down for a nap less than half an hour ago, so he'd be wide-awake to enjoy the festivities when Nick arrived in a couple of hours.

Wiping her hands on her apron, she turned for the

pantry, pulled open the door and looked inside for the bag of potatoes she'd picked up at the grocery store yesterday evening, but she didn't see them there.

"Shoot." She'd probably forgotten to get them out of the trunk of the car last night when she'd pulled in with a sleepy Caleb, and not enough hands to take on the entire load at once.

Spotting her keys on the bar next to her purse and her cell phone, she snagged them and headed for the garage. In the utility room, she flipped the light switch next to the door and pulled it open, sending a shard of illumination knifing into the dark garage.

Reaching back around, she flipped the switch a couple of times, but the lightbulb wouldn't come on. It must have burned out at some point while she was gone.

Aggravated, she pushed the utility-room door wide-open so she could see into the windowless garage, selected the trunk key and headed for the rear of the car.

Bending close to the lock, so she could see it better, she fit the key in and popped the latch.

A hand, cold and brutal, slammed over her mouth, sealing the air in her lungs.

The copper-penny tang of blood leaked across her tongue where her lower lip split against her teeth.

She struggled to free herself, but his other hand clamped onto her exposed throat and he began to squeeze.

"I came all this way, and you didn't even invite me to dinner, did you?"

Horror leeched from her bones as the sound of Rodney Marshall's voice penetrated her eardrums.

She screamed into his thick palm and lashed out with everything she had.

He retaliated, ramming a balled fist straight into her solar plexus so hard, she couldn't pull in her next breath.

"Save it, bitch," he whispered. "I'm just getting started."

He grabbed a handful of her hair and yanked her away from the open trunk of the car and back into the house.

NICK STARED into the bakery cooler at an array of pies, some of which he'd never even heard of. What the heck was a marionberry anyway? He wished he'd had the foresight to ask what kind Grace liked, but at least he knew she'd enjoy the bundle of fresh gerbera daisies he held in his good hand. He had Faith Scott to thank for that tip.

A wave of uneasiness surged inside of him and ebbed along his nerve endings. He discounted it and decided to call her and ask.

He shoved the flowers, stem-end first into his sling, and took his cell phone out of his pocket. He had another hour before he was due at Grace's place, but maybe he'd head over early with the right kind of pie.

Working his thumb into the phone, he flipped it open and punched in her number. Five rings later, his call rolled over to voice mail and he left a message, then hung up.

Odd. He was absolutely certain she was home right now.

Leaving the flowers in next to his cast, he picked up the marionberry pie and headed for the checkout counter.

GRACE LISTENED TO CALEB whimper behind his bedroom door and closed her eyes, silently thanking God that

Rodney Marshall had locked him inside using the belt from her bathrobe, by tying one end to each opposing doorknob of their bedrooms, so he couldn't get out.

A least he didn't have to see the horror unfolding in the kitchen, as Rodney drew the turkey-carving knife across her throat for a second time, just deep enough to draw blood.

"You need to pay for what you did, Grace. Troy didn't deserve to die like a dog. You got away with murder, but I can't let you do that. What kind of man would I be if I let his death go unchallenged?"

She swallowed hard against the terror inside of her, feeling rivulets of her own blood make tracks down her chest and soak into her bra.

"It was an accident, Rodney. I swear I never meant to hurt him."

He turned dark eyes on her, and for an instant she thought she saw some sense of sanity warm them, but then it vanished and he raised the knife again.

NICK FIRED UP the Tahoe's engine, but didn't pull out of the grocery store lot. Instead he reached in his pocket and pulled out his cell phone again. Working it open, he hit Redial and let it ring. Again his call went unanswered and rolled over to Grace's voice mail. He didn't leave a message this time.

Something was wrong.

He could accept her missing his call once. Maybe she'd been taking the bird out of the oven, or stirring the mashed potatoes, but twice?

Nick closed his phone, put his rig in Drive and gunned it out of the parking lot.

GRACE LISTENED to her cell phone beep for a second time, signaling a missed call.

She stared at it from where Rodney Marshall had tied her to one of the dining-room chairs with her hands behind her back, bound in duct tape, her ankles taped to the front legs, and a thick strip across her mouth, so she'd shut up.

Fighting against the bonds, she tried to work her wrists free, but he'd cinched them tight. She couldn't move, much less feel her fingers anymore. Her brain was numb.

Where was Nick?

The clock on the dining room wall read 6:23 p.m. Rodney had assured her she'd be dead by seven o'clock.

"Fire. Fire cleanses, Grace. Did you know that?" Rodney asked her as he came through the utility-room door with a red gas can in his hand. "It burns evidence, too. The cops can't prosecute what they don't have."

He casually tipped the can over and drizzled the floor of the kitchen with it, then worked his way into the living room. "Sure wish I could stay to enjoy dinner with you, Grace. I remember how good your turkey was, but I've gotta be back to work the day after tomorrow. I've got a hell of a drive in front of me."

Terror sliced through her as she watched him splash gasoline down the hallway outside of Caleb's bedroom door. He put the gas can down in front of it, and dug into his pocket to produce a book of matches.

He was going to burn them both alive?

Horror consumed her body and soul as she began to scream behind the suffocating tape over her mouth and rock her chair back and forth as hard as she could.

"It'll be over soon, Grace, but it won't be quick. I

want you to suffer like Troy suffered, with no one there to save your miserable life."

He stepped back through the living room and moved toward the front door.

"He was my brother, Grace. You didn't have to murder him. You had a choice that night, just like I have a choice right now."

He tore a match out of the book and closed the cover. "I kind of feel bad about Caleb, but he's suffering, too, with his disease. He'll be better off leaving this world with you."

Rodney turned the knob and pulled the front door open a crack, then struck the match in his hand.

Grace watched in terror as it flamed to life, then tried to make sense of the explosion of blood and matter that suddenly shot out of Rodney Marshall's forehead in slow motion.

She watched the match drop from his fingertips and extinguish before it hit the floor at his feet.

Rodney Marshall fell forward, as the echo of gunfire assaulted her eardrums.

Reality smacked into her brain as her chair finally tipped over and she hit the floor.

Her world went black.

NICK LOWERED HIS PISTOL and jammed his boot against the partially open front door of Grace's condo that now had two large-bore pistol rounds drilled through it.

The overwhelming stink of gasoline immediately put him on alert as he stared down at Rodney Marshall, sprawled facedown on the living-room floor minus the back of his skull.

He spotted Grace in the dining room, as Sheriff Hale charged up the walk and stepped in behind him.

Several deputies followed, as Nick hurried to where Grace lay strapped to a chair with her eyes closed.

"Get an ambulance, Sheriff. She needs help."

Nick's heart squeezed inside his chest, and he went to his knees next to Grace and touched her face.

"What did he do to you, Grace?" Nick's breath caught in his throat as he worked the tape off her mouth. He watched her open her eyes and she looked at him.

"Caleb!" Panic set him back. He climbed to his feet and spotted the crude lock Marshall had put on the bedroom doors.

"Caleb!" He could hear him crying just behind the door. "Caleb, can you hear me? It's Mister Nick. Everything's going to be okay."

A deputy was already in the process of untying the belt locking him inside, away from the ugly scene outside, and he wanted to keep it that way.

"Can you sit with him until we get Grace and Marshall out of here? I don't want him traumatized any more than he has already been. He doesn't need to see any of this."

The deputy nodded, finished untying the knot and slipped into Caleb's room to comfort the distraught child.

Nick hurried back to Grace's side and set the chair upright, listening to her pull in a deep breath.

"Caleb?"

"He's okay, Grace. An officer is keeping him in his room until we take you both out of here."

"Marshall?"

"Dead. I had the shots and I took them. I should have killed the SOB weeks ago."

The sound of sirens filled the air and Grace closed her eyes.

Secure in the knowledge that Rodney Marshall would never hurt them again.

Chapter Seventeen

Grace stood next to Governor Lila Lockhart in front of the Twin Harts Mansion, and stared at the row of television cameras amassed and aimed at them both.

Her body was a tangle of nerves, but she'd been instructed to stand alert and smile. All responses she knew she could handle.

Glancing past the lenses and faces behind them, she settled her gaze on Nick, where he stood looking strong and handsome in the circular driveway just beyond the madness.

She'd taken his advice this morning, and worn her black turtleneck sweater to hide the ugly evidence of Rodney Marshall's assault on her, and the questions that would naturally be generated by it. Soon enough the story would come to light.

"Good morning," Lila announced as she stepped behind the impromptu podium set up just in front of the main doors leading into the Twin Harts mansion.

It seemed a fitting and comfortable setting for an announcement about family, and she planned to take full advantage of it. The political polls in the weeks to come would be her indicator of where she went from this day forward, but she knew in her heart of hearts that right was right, and she was going to do the right thing. Let the chips fall where they may, even if it damaged her bid for the presidency.

"When I was twenty-two years old, I got pregnant as a college student, and at the urging of my family, I gave that child, a beautiful baby girl named Grace, up for adoption to a loving family."

Grace kept her focus on Nick, pulling strength from the reassuring nod he gave her as she listened to Lila relate the story of how they'd come to this point in time. It didn't matter that some of the facts were glossed over, or went unmentioned. All that mattered now was that Caleb was going to receive his transplant. He was going to live.

"And so, I will be flying to Texas Children's Hospital in Houston to donate bone marrow to my grandson in December."

A burst of applause erupted, followed by an onslaught of questions from the bank of reporters.

"I'm sorry, but I won't be taking any questions this morning. I ask that you respect my family's privacy and allow us to get to know each other far removed from the press."

"Grace." Lila took her hand, and together they entered the front doors of the house.

Once inside, Bailey hurried forward and wrapped her arms around Grace. "Welcome to the family."

She hugged Bailey back, and turned as Nick slipped inside and moved toward her through the crush of people in the gallery. All she wanted was to feel his arms around her now, and forever, and to head for the ranch where she could relax and heal.

"Nick told us what happened last night, Grace,"

Parker said as he gave her a bear hug. "We're glad you're okay."

"You must have been terrified," Bailey added, as she took hold of Grace's hand and gave it a squeeze. "If you need to talk, I'm here for you. We're family now. Remember that."

"Thank you both."

The couple left hand in hand, and headed for the dining room, where Grace knew the governor had lunch prepared.

"Grace," Lila said after she broke from the small circle of advisors who'd encased her the moment they'd come back into the mansion. "You did a wonderful job, dear."

Nick singled Grace out, and rode to her rescue, as he moved in next to her and pressed his hand into the small of her back.

"I've got my staff dissecting my campaign schedule for an opening in early December where the transplant can take place."

"Thank you, Lila. You have no idea how much this means to Caleb and me, and Nick."

The governor's smile faded as she reached up and touched her cheek. "I heard about what happened last night. It's a good thing Agent Cavanaugh showed up when he did."

"Yes, it is, and about that, Lila." She wasn't sure she was comfortable calling her "mother" just yet, but in time she knew she would. "I'm exhausted. I'd like to pass on lunch and go home if you don't mind."

"Certainly, dear. Get some rest. You've had a harrowing experience. We'll speak after the weekend."

Grace nodded as Lila pulled her into her arms and hugged her tightly.

A man in a suit and geek glasses hurried toward them with a broad grin on his face. "Excuse me, Governor, but the blogosphere is going crazy, and it's all positive reaction so far."

Lila stepped back. "How is that even feasible, Mr. Olson? I haven't been away from the cameras and microphone for more than ten minutes."

In awe of the speed at which her message had been received, deciphered and redistributed, Lila excused herself and walked away, headed presumably for a peek at the response her announcement was generating in cyberspace.

Nick took Grace's hand and led her out the back way to where he'd parked the Tahoe beyond the eyes of the press, so they could make a clean getaway without drawing attention.

He didn't relax until he had her inside the vehicle and they were pulling out onto the main road for the drive back to the ranch, where Faith and Matteo had volunteered to look after Caleb until their return.

"You did well back there. How are you holding up?"

"Well? I didn't say a single word, as instructed, and I managed to avoid a deer-in-the-headlights stare into all of the cameras."

"Mission accomplished." He wanted to reach over and take her hand, but he needed his single grip on the steering wheel to keep the Tahoe on the road.

"I talked to Sheriff Hale this morning. He agreed to come out to the ranch on Monday morning to take our statements. There won't be any need to make an appearance at the station."

She sucked in a deep breath and let it out slowly. "Thank you for buying me a small reprieve. I'm not sure I'm ready to relive that."

"You're welcome."

Silence encircled them as Nick spotted the turnoff leading into the back of the ranch, across the open range and to the back of the house. Slowing, he pulled onto the narrow dirt road and crossed the cattle guard, as Grace leaned forward in curiosity and stared through the front windshield.

"Where are we?"

"The back route into the ranch."

A smile tugged her lips, the first true one he'd seen all morning. "I have our picnic lunch in the back. Caleb made it for me this morning."

She gazed over at him. "PB and J?"

"Yeah."

"I love those," she whispered.

Nick's heart squeezed inside his chest as he spotted the scrub oak where they'd picnicked before. "This looks like the place." He parked the Tahoe. "Stay put. Let me get it set up."

"Okay."

He climbed out of the rig, went around to the back and got out the picnic supplies. On the horizon, he could see the ranch house in the distance, and the flash of Matteo's 4Runner as he pulled through the back gate headed in their direction.

Under the scrub oak, he spread the blanket, put down the basket and returned to the truck, but Grace had already climbed out and was pulling deep breaths of the sage-scented air into her lungs.

Grinning up at him, she reached out and touched his

arm. "I love it here, Nick. It's so peaceful. It's just what I need right now. I just wish Caleb were here to enjoy it with us."

He followed her over to the blanket, took her hand and pulled her to him, feeling her excitement encase him, as well. Leaning down, he brushed his lips against hers, feeling the heated response he craved as it came to life in her body. Savoring the moment, he broke the connection, dug into his pocket and pulled out the ring.

Going down on one knee, he looked up at her, seeing the realization in her heavenly blue eyes. Her hand went to her heart, the exact place he always wanted to be.

"Grace Marshall, I love you, and I can't get through this life without you, and Caleb."

Grace's heart filled with happiness that threatened to take her to her knees if she didn't do something. Leaning forward, she kissed Nick on the mouth before he could get another word out, then pulled back.

"Yes," she whispered, going to her knees next to him.

"Marry me, then?"

She steered him down onto the blanket and together they lay back against the scrub oak.

"Left hand, please." Nick jockeyed to the right so he could slip the engagement ring on her finger.

In the background he heard the vehicle come to a stop behind them.

"I love you both, you know." He met Grace's gaze. "I want to be your husband, and Caleb's father."

"Mister Nick!"

The sound of his little guy's voice put a knot in his chest, as he turned to wave to Matteo, who released Caleb and climbed back into the 4Runner for the drive back to the ranch house.

"Mister Nick!"

"You're going to be a great addition to the Daddy Corps," she whispered, watching her tiny son charge forward onto the blanket and pile onto Nick's lap.

"I wanna eat," Caleb said, reaching over to dig in the picnic basket. "Can we eat now?"

"Yeah, buddy."

Grace reached out and squeezed his hand, then helped Caleb spread lunch out on the blanket between them, before he bit into his peanut-butter-and-jelly sandwich.

"Mister Nick," he asked, picking a Goldfish out of his baggie and popping it into his mouth, "what's a wedding ring?"

Nick glanced up at Grace and watched a sweet smile pull up her perfect lips.

"Well, Caleb, I'm going to tell you, but then you'll have to call me Dad from now on. Do you think you can do that?"

"Yep," he said as he stood up and locked his arms around Nick's neck.

* * * * *

SUSPENSE

Heartstopping stories of intrigue and mystery—
where true love always triumphs.

◈ Harlequin®

INTRIGUE

COMING NEXT MONTH
AVAILABLE DECEMBER 6, 2011

#1317 BABY BATTALION
Daddy Corps
Cassie Miles

#1318 DADDY BOMBSHELL
Situation: Christmas
Lisa Childs

#1319 DADE
The Lawmen of Silver Creek Ranch
Delores Fossen

#1320 TOP GUN GUARDIAN
Brothers in Arms
Carol Ericson

#1321 NANNY 911
The Precinct: SWAT
Julie Miller

#1322 BEAR CLAW BODYGUARD
Bear Claw Creek Crime Lab
Jessica Andersen

You can find more information on upcoming Harlequin® titles,
free excerpts and more at www.HarlequinInsideRomance.com.

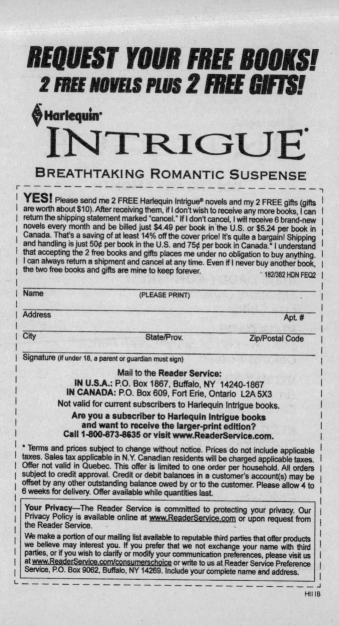

*Lucy Flemming and Ross Mitchell shared a magical,
sexy Christmas weekend together six years ago.
This Christmas, history may repeat itself when they find
themselves stranded in a major snowstorm…
and alone at last.*

Read on for a sneak peek from
IT HAPPENED ONE CHRISTMAS
by Leslie Kelly.

Available December 2011, only from Harlequin® Blaze™.

EYEING THE GRAY, THICK SKY through the expansive wall of
windows, Lucy began to pack up her photography gear.
The Christmas party was winding down, only a dozen or so
people remaining on this floor, which had been transformed
from cubicles and meeting rooms to a holiday funland. She
smiled at those nearest to her, then, seeing the glances at her
silly elf hat, she reached up to tug it off her head.

Before she could do it, however, she heard a voice. A
deep, male voice—smooth and sexy, and so not Santa's.

"I appreciate you filling in on such short notice. I've
heard you do a terrific job."

Lucy didn't turn around, letting her brain process what
she was hearing. Her whole body had stiffened, the hairs on
the back of her neck standing up, her skin tightening into
tiny goose bumps. Because that voice sounded so familiar.
Impossibly familiar.

It can't be.

"It sounds like the kids had a great time."

Unable to stop herself, Lucy began to turn around,
wondering if her ears—and all her other senses—were
deceiving her. After all, six years was a long time, the mind

could play tricks. What were the odds that she'd bump into *him*, here? And today of all days. December 23.

Six years exactly. Was that really possible?

One look—and the accompanying frantic thudding of her heart—and she knew her ears and brain were working just fine. Because it was *him*.

"Oh, my God," he whispered, shocked, frozen, staring as thoroughly as she was. "Lucy?"

She nodded slowly, not taking her eyes off him, wondering why the years had made him even more attractive than ever. It didn't seem fair. Not when she'd spent the past six years thinking he must have started losing that thick, golden-brown hair, or added a spare tire to that trim, muscular form.

No.

The man was gorgeous. Truly, without-a-doubt, mouth-wateringly handsome, every bit as hot as he'd been the first time she'd laid eyes on him. She'd been twenty-two, he one year older.

They'd shared an amazing holiday season.

And had never seen one another again.

Until now.

Find out what happens in
IT HAPPENED ONE CHRISTMAS
by Leslie Kelly.
Available December 2011, only from Harlequin® Blaze™